DAVID GRAHAM
THE NEW GUN

OTHER BOOKS by PAUL L. THOMPSON

Shorty Thompson, U S Marshall
Marshall Thompson, Vol. 1

Silver Of The Black Range
Marshall Thompson, Vol. 2

Willow Lane
Marshall Thompson, Vol. 3

Marshall Thompson, Vol. 4
(In Production Re-design)

Revenge In Tascosa
Marshall Thompson, Vol. 5

Ride Hard For Raydao
Marshall Thompson, Vol. 6

Malpais
Marshall Thompson, Vol. 7

Children Of The West
Marshall Thompson, Vol. 8

Killers And Horse Thieves
Marshall Thompson, Vol. 9

The Littlest Gun
Marshall Thompson, Vol. 10

A Mother's Wrath
Marshall Thompson, Vol. 11

When Preaching Is Hell
Marshall Thompson, Vol. 12

Brothers Of The West
Marshall Thompson, Vol. 13

Young Jesse Owens
Marshall Thompson, Vol. 14

Women Of The West Did Survive
Marshall Thompson, Vol. 15

The Last Gun in Town
Marshall Thompson, Vol. 16

The Long Chase for Justice
Marshall Thompson, Vol. 17

The Wrong Man Again
Marshall Thompson, Vol. 18

The Young Trackers
Marshall Thompson, Vol. 19

This Mountain Is Mine
Marshall Thompson, Vol. 20

Janice McCord
Marshall Thompson, Vol. 21

Whiskers McPherson & Gabriel O'Grady
Marshall Thompson, Vol. 22

Killing of Outlaws
Marshall Thompson, Vol. 23

Before I Die
Marshall Thompson, Vol. 24

The Martin Boys
Marshall Thompson, Vol. 25

Cowboy Cody Strickland
Marshall Thompson, Vol. 26

Please Don't Leave Me
Marshall Thompson, Vol. 27

DAVID GRAHAM
THE NEW GUN

BY

PAUL L. THOMPSON

David Graham, The New Gun
All Rights Reserved © 2012 by Paul L. Thompson

Book Design by Robert T. Garcia / Garcia Publishing Services, www.gpsdesign.net
Cover Photo of Chloride, NM Copyright © 2000 Geronimo Trail Scenic Byway Inc..

J Published in 2012 by
JADA Press (www.JadaPress.com)
Jacksonville, FL
JADA USA

ISBN: 978-0-9848365-2-9

Printed in the United States of America

Dedication

This novel of fiction is dedicated to Kathy and William, (Bill) Cushing.

They are the owners of the Burger Boy Café in Cedar Crest, New Mexico. Though Bill has past on, Kathy works her butt off, carrying on what they started. No one alive could have better friends. I miss Bill every day, but know he looks over my shoulder as I write my novels. Kathy loves my novels, as did Bill, and she is still one of my dearest, most treasured fans. May the Great Spirit look after her, all the days of her life.

FOREWORD

In the small mining town of Chloride, New Mexico Territory, four young men rob the bank and shoot the teller. As they ride down the street leaving town, a teen age boy and girl see their faces. Several shot were fired their way, the girl went down.

David Graham knew he had to get a gun to protect himself and others. He wasn't worth a crap with a pistol, but with a rifle he was among the best in the country. A rifle couldn't be carried in his hands all the time. What he needed was a new gun. Yes, a new kind of gun.

Leo Patterson, a close friend owned and ran the livery and blacksmith shop. An idea came to him, so he asked if David would leave his rifle with him for awhile.

When Leo was through, a new gun was built. Outlaws and gun manufacturers wanted that rifle and the holster that held it to David's right leg. Outlaws knew they would be unbeatable. Gun manufacturers knew they could make millions with this new gun. It would be the best rifle/pistol to come out since the repeater.

Leo's father, owner of the Patterson Firearms Company sent two men all the way from Patterson, New Jersey to get that rifle no matter the cost. Leo's father turned out to be just as greedy as Leo remembered and knew he was.

CHAPTER ONE

Seventeen year old David Graham stepped from his father's grocery and mercantile store with the bank deposit in his hand. Pretty Margret Thomas was on the wagon seat beside her father, as they pulled to a stop in front of the store.

David smiled, "Good morning Mister Thomas, and a good morning to you Margret."

Mister Thomas stepped down and got the bridle weight, dropping it on the ground in front of the horses. This gave David plenty of time to help Margret from the wagon.

As they stepped to the walkway, David started to turn toward the bank that was down the street about a block. "Yer not coming back inside?" Mister Thomas asked, as he took Margret by her right elbow.

"Naw, but I'll be right back and help load what you need. Pa is inside, but I have to get over to the bank."

Where her father couldn't see, Margret gave David a very sweet smile and asked her father, "Papa, would it be okay if I walked with David?"

"I suppose so, but you young'uns hurry. I have a lot of work to do today."

Mister Thomas walked on inside the store, as Margret and David walked across the street. Margret wanted to reach and hold David's hand, but knew better. People would talk and she nor David were ready for that.

"Are you going to the picnic this Sunday?" She looked up into his eyes and almost stumbled on a small rock.

David grabbed her and smiled as he stood her back on her feet. "Yes, if yer gonna be…" Four young horsemen slowly rode past with one of them making a wise remark about Margret's rear end.

David started to bow up, but Margret caught his arm. "Let it go David, those boys are wearing guns."

As they stepped to the walkway, in front of them was the dress shop. "Oh look David! What a beautiful Easter dress. Do you have time for us to go in and look at it?"

David quickly looked all around. "Naw, fellers don't go in no dress shop. But you go ahead I'll just wait right here."

"Yer silly but thank you, I'll only be a moment." She walked inside with David looking all around to see who might catch him standing in front of a woman's dress shop.

He looked back at his father's store but didn't see the wagon being loaded. His eyes jerked toward the bank as a gunshot was heard and three men came running from the bank to a waiting man holding horses.

People stepped from doorways as four men kicked their horses into an all out run up the street. Just before they got even with David, Margret stepped from the dress shop. She put her hand to her mouth and shouted, "David that is the same boys that rode past us a moment…"

Three shots came their way, one knocking Margret to the walkway. David saw the grin on the shooters face as they rode around a bend and from sight. He grabbed Margret up in his arms and walked swiftly toward the doctor's office.

Bob Graham and Seth Thomas had stepped from the store to see what all the shooting was about. As the riders rode past with horses in an all out run and out of sight, Seth asked, "I wonder what that was all about."

Bob was looking down the street and saw David walking with Margret in his arms. "Good Lord Tom, Margret!"

He was pointing down the street at David just as he disappeared into the doctor's office. Both men ran, leaving no one in the store. As they rushed through the door, Doctor Williams was leaning over Margret.

David was standing there, looking as if he didn't have one drop of blood left in his face. "Pa, Mister Thomas, those boys shot Margret for no cause."

Mister Thomas walked over to the table beside the doctor, as he was putting several drops of a liquid from a small bottle on a clean cloth and held it over Margret's face. "Seth, she'll be alright, but I need you three to get out of here for a bit. I'll call you after I get this hole cleaned and sewed up where that slug went."

By this time the whole town was in an up roar, in front of the bank. Sheriff Dobbs and his deputy stepped from the bank. "I want a posse ready to ride in five minutes!"

Men grabbed any horse they saw standing at hitch rails that was wearing a saddle. The posse rode from town in a cloud of dust. Men peeked inside the bank to see Mister Aldan kneeling over his teller. One of the men hollered inside, "Want me to get the doc?"

"No need, Lee is dead. But you could go get Mister Ford as he can get him ready for burying."

"I'll do that right now, Sir."

It was almost an hour before the doctor came out of the room and got Mister Thomas. "You can come in now Seth, but she won't be awake for another hour or so."

"How is she Doc? She's gonna be alright, ain't she?"

"Yes she'll be fine, but it'll take time healing. She has a good sized hole in her left side just above her hip bone."

"She'll still be able to walk, won't she?"

"Oh sure, she'll just have a scar where that bullet went in and came out. It hit no bone. Now I want her to stay right here at least until morning to make sure it didn't hit nothing vital. Then I'll see if I think it will be alright for you to move her and take her home."

Mister Thomas walked back to David and Bob. "She's

gonna be alright. David, did you see them fellers good what shot my Margret?"

"Oh yes Sir! Me an Margret saw um twice. When they was riding up the street, then after they robbed the bank. If Margret hadn't gone with me she wouldn't been shot."

Mister Thomas put his hand on David's shoulder. "Yes Son, but if she hadn't gone with you, you'd been in that bank when it was robbed. You might'a got killed."

Dick and Albert Boggs are nineteen and twenty year old brothers, as are Edgar and Jeff Nibbs. All four boys had been friends and outlaws since Jeff was old enough to kill and rob his first man of forty-five cents.

They had looked the town of Chloride and its bank over for a week. Only two at a time went in unnoticed and checked everything over, including the sheriff's office while the other two traced out an escape route. After robbing the bank, they knew which way to ride and not get caught by no posse.

They had been living in an abandoned mine southwest of here, on the east side of Diamond Peak for over six months. The well hidden location let them rob banks and stagecoaches all over the New Mexico Territory. They knew posses would get tired after a few days and most would go back home. Well maybe the sheriff and a couple of real do-gooders would hang in awhile longer, now that a teller was killed. That shouldn't have happened, Dick looked worried.

They always rode in the opposite direction of their hideout until they were sure of no longer being chased. After a couple miles of hard riding, they pulled the horses back to an easy, long lope.

Dick, being the oldest was looked up to and the other three knew he was in charge. He slowed his horse to a walk and took his canteen from the saddle horn. After a long drink, he turned his head toward Edgar. "Edgar, why in the hell did you shoot that right pretty little gal?"

"Wadn't trying to shoot her! I's trying for that kid with her. He saw ever one of us and could tell who we is."

"Now how in the hell could he do that? He don't know us and we don't got no papers out on us. To beat that I thought you was a better shot than to go an shoot some girl."

"Damn it we was running our horses! And just maybe one day he might could tell who we is, now that I shot his sister. Wosh I'd got him too."

"Now don't you think that little girl saw as much as him and would'a talked? They was together both times we saw um. This changes how we do things."

"Well yeah, but I wouldn't shot her no way."

"Bull crap! That's who you shot! The boy is alive and well. Just forget it we've got some riding to do. I'd bet that sheriff has a posse all worked up by now and is on our trail."

After a few more fast miles Albert called over to Dick. "How much do you think we got?"

"Not nigh what we could'a if Jeff hadn't shot that teller. We still hadn't got to that open vault."

Jeff almost screamed, "Damn it Dick, I thought he was going for a gun!"

"That was the second cash drawer, dummy!"

"I know that now, we'll just have to go back one day real soon and get what's in that vault. It's gotta be a lot."

"We're gonna, but it shor's hell won't be all that soon. That boy and banker saw us right good. We'll give um time to forget all about us. That'll take time. Sides that, there's a hell of a lot more banks around we ain't robbed one time, yet."

Instead of riding the stage road east toward Monticello, they cut most too due south and would stay this direction until they came to the Seco Creek. They would follow it a few miles southeast before cutting straight east for Las Palomas. They would be at the Rio Grande and could ride in any direction from there and not be caught.

With horses in a run, the Posse had gone past where four horses cut south. They rode on down the stage road almost a mile when one of the men hollered over at the sheriff, "Hey Sheriff, there ain't no tracks we're follering!"

All the horses were brought to a sliding halt and everyone started looking around for tracks. After several minutes, while cussing under his breath, Sheriff Dobbs hollered out, "We've gotta back track! Ever body keep yore eyes open! We don't know if they went north er south!"

The ride back toward Chloride was slow, taking a good half hour. About a hundred yards before coming into the curve just before town, a rider called everyone over. "Here they went south on four horses in a damn big hurry."

The sheriff looked over at him saying, "Hell yes they was in a run! You would be to if you just robbed a bank and killed a teller!"

"Yeah, an then went an shot little Margret Thomas."

Sheriff Dobbs jerked back on the reins, stopping his horse. "What? Who shot Margret?"

"Them fellers we're chasing went an done it."

"Why wasn't I told?"

"I just found out when I grabbed this horse from in front of the grocery. Mister Graham told me."

"Alright, let's ride! We know what kind of men we're after. We catch um, shoot um on sight." They headed south at a pretty good clip. The sheriff knew they were now a good hour or better behind and didn't want to ruin one of the posse horses. A slow steady pace must be held.

It was a good thirty miles from Chloride to Las Palomas and even pushing the horses hard without killing them, it took the four young outlaws well over two hours to get there. They pulled to a stop in front of the grocery. "We've gotta have us some beans, hardtacks, jerky and coffee. Edgar, you an Albert get these horses watered. Jeff come on, we'll get the grub."

Edgar could tell Dick was worried and in a hurry. There had been two killings on this robbery and that would put the law after them for a good while. It might even be months before things died down again.

Twenty minutes later they were riding the west bank of the Rio Grande. Edgar looked over at Dick, but first thought of what he was going to say. After a few minutes he got up the nerve. "Dick, yer worried about this posse, huh?"

"Yes I sure as hell am, Jeff shooting that teller, then you going and shooting that girl. I don't know about that sheriff, but if he's a blood hound we could be in real trouble."

"Yeah but we know this Territory like nobody else. We'll leave him no trail to foller."

Dick looked over at him then cut his horse into the water. "We'll ride water as long as it don't get too awful deep. At least it'll slow um up."

All day they slowly rode on while looking over their shoulders at their back trail. They had past the Hillsboro, Kingston stage road and were about twelve miles north of Hatch. Sundown, but well before dark they rode into a grove of trees along the river bank and set up camp for the night. Dick and Edgar unsaddled and hobbled horses while Jeff and Albert gathered wood and started a fire.

With a plate of beans and a cup of coffee Albert asked, "Where are we headed?"

"Las Cruces, Mesilla and maybe on down to El Paso."

"Damn, that's the farthest we've ever had to ride after a job. Think that posse is still coming?"

"Yep, and so pissed off they want'a kill somebody. We might ride upon that big mountain that's north of El Paso and watch our back trail for a good while. If we're still being follered, we'll not stop in El Paso, just go on over into Mexico. Maybe that sheriff won't foller us there."

Dick looked over as Jeff started taking the hobbles off the horses. "What'er you doing?"

"Taking off these damn hobbles an tying these horses. It's a hell of a lot quicker untying by jerking a knot than taking off hobbles if we have to leave here in a hurry."

"Yeah yer right, good thinking."

* * * *

Sheriff Dobbs stopped his posse right at the Hillsboro, Kingston stage road cut off and camped for the night. Sal Benton got a cup of coffee, leaned back against his saddle and asked, "Melton, how far back would you guess we are?"

"Two, maybe three hours at the most. By looking at their tracks I can tell they're pushing harder than we are. We're losing ground. This might be a long chase unless they stop somewhere and get drunk on that bank money."

"Where would you think that might be?"

"Mesilla, er Las Cruces I'm guessing. You know we was just plain lucky picking up their tracks again after they rode out of the river. I'd say they have been chased before."

"Think they're headed for Mexico?"

"Could be, that's the way they're riding."

"We ain't gonna go into Mexico after um if they are, are we?" Sal didn't like nothing about Mexico.

"Naw, that Mexican Government frowns on U S law riding across their border. They'd sooner shoot us than any outlaw. I think that's cause they are all outlaws."

Well before sunup everyone was on the road toward Las Cruces. Dick kicked his horse into a long ground eating lope. He had a feeling that posse wouldn't stop as soon as all the others had. Before this job, if caught, they would have just spent a few years in prison. Now they would hang. He felt sorry for the teller and that girl, and he didn't want to get caught and swing for something he didn't do.

They made it to Hatch before eight-o-clock and knew

by pushing even harder they would be in Las Cruces before nightfall. Seven miles south of Hatch, Edger's horse pulled up lame. It was limping bad and couldn't go on.

"Jeff, Edgar will ride double with you an Albert can carry that saddle. We'll get another horse in Las Cruces."

Albert helped unsaddle the lame horse while saying, "Boy howdy, this is shor gonna slow us down."

Dick looked over his shoulder, back toward Hatch. "Yeah, but we've been pushing so that'll give us a dab more time. Least I hope so, as I'd hate getting in a gunfight with a posse anywhere around here. Too damn open."

Four miles farther down, they came in sight of a farm. Pulling the horses up, Dick said they might could get a horse here. Slowly they rode into the yard and called out. An elderly Spanish fellow walked out of the low doorway. *"Si,* something you wants?"

"Yeah, how about selling us that horse over there in that corral?" It wasn't a very good looking horse, but it would do.

"Naw *Senor,* I can not do that, he is the only one I haves. But my cousin Orlando, what lives just across the river would sell you one of his. He has many."

"Thanks." They rode over and crossed the river in belly deep water. The horses didn't have to swim. The farm house here looked as the other one did, built out of Adobe with a low door and small windows.

Hollering right loud brought a man from a small goat shed. He looked the men over and wished he had his old rifle in his hands. *"Si,* what's you want?"

"Looking to buy a horse."

"Si, that bay gilding I want twenty pesos."

"How about ten?"

"Naw *Senor,* I no do that. Twenty pesos."

"Okay, how old is he?"

"Four years old and broke really good to ride."

Edgar threw his saddle and bridle on that horse and stepped into the saddle. "Let's ride."

The horse proved to be a good one and they made good time the rest of the way to Las Cruces. Going straight to the livery, Jeff asked why they were leaving the horses here. "They need grain and hay. "We'll get us a room and leave before daylight."

After stalling the horses, they walked down the street to the first saloon. Within an hour, they were in a gunfight with two loud mouthed Mexicans that did not like Gringos. The Mexicans were dead in less than a half second and the four boys had to back out of that saloon with guns in their hands. Grinning, Edgar grabbed a full bottle of tequila from the end of the bar.

Going to the livery, they got their horses and headed south in a long lope. It was dark with a half moon shining as they cut off the road and camped for the night on the west bank of the Rio Grande.

CHAPTER TWO

After morning coffee and jerky, Dick and the boys cut east at Mesquite, headed for the tall mountain just north of El Paso. This south end of the Organ Mountains was steep, rocky and hard on horses. It was a good two or three thousand feet higher than the Rio Grande Valley.

Sheriff Dobbs and his posse rode into Las Cruces before mid-morning on tired horses. After getting a bite to eat, they went over to the sheriff's office, asking if four strangers had rode into town last night or this morning. That was all he wanted to know. When the sheriff told him of the two dead Mexicans in that saloon, Sheriff Dobbs took a deep breath and sat down.

"Well Sheriff, it looks like them killers give us the slip and are headed for Mexico."

"They'd better be. What'er you gonna do?"

"Head back home. No need in riding another forty-five miles to find out what I already know. Maybe one day they'll come riding back into Chloride."

"That'd be unlikely being as they killed that teller and shot a girl. Any posters out on um?"

"Naw, but if the banker and David Graham can give a good enough description, I'll have some made up and sent out by stagecoach."

"Are you heading back right now?"

"Naw, the men need to rest up a bit and so do the horses. We'll leave come morning."

* * * *

Margret had to stay at the doctor's office for two days.

She was still bleeding a small amount from her wounds and the bandages had to be changed twice a day. David visited her every chance he got.

On the third morning, Seth pulled his wagon to a stop in front of the doctor's office. There was bedding all laid out in the back and even a pillow. David had seen him drive by the store, and hurried over to the doc's office to see Margret one more time.

"Here David, give me a hand carrying her to the wagon." She didn't weigh much more than a hundred pounds, they just wanted to be very careful.

The doctor smiled saying, "You were a very good patient. Now you have your pa bring you back in a week. No, don't do that, it'll be best if I just came out there." He started to turn back to his office but stopped and said, "Seth, you be sure and keep those bandages clean. If either hole starts getting red, you come and get me at once, don't put it off."

"Thanks Doc. What do I owe you?"

"No hurry, take care of it the next time you are in town."

David stood at the end of the wagon looking down at Margret. "Mister Thomas, it would be no trouble me going with you to help Margret into the house."

"My goodness, I never thought of getting her in the house. I'll wait while you get your horse."

"Naw you go ahead, I'll catch up."

Seth Thomas had a small farm and ranch two miles south of town. He raised a few head of cattle and farmed. His chickens and milk cows, hogs and garden supplied him and Margret with most of their food. His wife had past on three years ago when Margret was thirteen. Several times he had thought about selling out and maybe going to work in the mines, as they sure paid more than farming and ranching.

Three quarters of an hour later, Margret was in her bed

being pampered more than a new born colt. Her father fluffed the pillow, asking if she was comfortable.

"Papa, I'm fine. Now you go on, I know you've been putting off work because of me."

He smiled at his beautiful daughter. "Alright, I'll take care of the horses but I'll be back in before I head to the field." He walked to the bedroom door but stopped and asked, "You coming. David?"

"Huh, oh yeah I gotta be getting back to the store. Bye Margret, I'll drop by tomorrow and see if you need anything." He gave her a smile and followed Mister Thomas into the yard.

"I sure want to thank you for your help, David."

"Yes Sir, I didn't mind at all." All the way back to town, he kept going over in his mind, what if he had a gun that day? Could he have prevented Margret from getting shot? He knew he was a very good shot with a rifle, as he had won the last two turkey shoots. But shooting a pistol? Naw, he'd only held a couple in his hands a few times, but never shot one.

As he rode past the little café, the owner, William Cushing was sweeping the walkway out front. Looking up as David approached, he called out. "David, why don't you and Bob drop by for dinner? Kathy has a mighty fine meal just about ready."

"Thanks Bill, we'll be over in a few minutes."

Tying the horse at the hitch rail in front of the store, he walked in and told his father Kathy had dinner just about ready. "Alright David, I'll put these boxes away while you take care of your horse and meet you over there."

Fifteen minutes later they walked into the café and found it almost full. Every table except one was taken. As they sit down, Bill came over with a pot of coffee and two cups. "Howdy Bob, what will y'all be having today?"

"I think I smell some of Kathy's pot roast."

"You sure do, will that be two bowls?"

"Yes and a few slices of that bread I can also smell."

Bill smiled as he walked back to the kitchen and handed the order to Kathy. Grabbing four filled bowls, he headed to a table over close to the front window.

As he set them on the table, three loud men walked in. Bill looked up saying, "A table will clear out in a couple of minutes and I'll clean it so you can sit down."

Henry and Oscar Beal was almost finished with their meal and waved to Bill for another cup of coffee. The men saw that saying, "That's alright, we'll just take that table."

"Fine, it'll only take a couple of minutes."

"Naw, we'll take it now! The man caught hold of the table cloth and jerked the plates and cups crashing to the floor. They all three laughed as Oscar and Henry jumped to their feet and stepped back.

Bill opened and closed his mouth a couple of times saying, "You men will sure as heck pay for that!"

"Why would we pay for cups and plates when we wadn't even gonna pay for the meal?"

"Get! I mean get and don't ever come in here thinking you can tear up my place and disturb my customers."

The man put his hand on Bill's chest and pushed hard, trying to shove him down. Bill took a couple steps back then busted the fellow's nose, knocking him to the floor. The two other men started to step in, but stopped when Kathy shoved a double barrel shotgun in their faces.

"My husband asked you fellers to leave! Best you did just that!" Kathy pulled both hammers to full cock.

The men helped their friend off the floor and toward the door. One of the loud mouths turned and said, "We'll damn sure be back!"

Kathy smiled, "I wouldn't do that if I was you. Next time the undertaker will carry you out. Nobody touches my Bill without being hurt somewhat."

Kathy went on back to the kitchen while Bill apologized to everyone. David laughed out loud, where most grown men and women just smiled. They already knew Bill, nor Kathy were pushovers. They protected what was theirs.

Bill kept bringing out bowls of pot roast as people came and went. Bob paid for their meal then walked to the kitchen door. "Kathy, yer still the best cook in the whole southwest."

"I know it Bob, but thanks for telling me."

As Bob and David got back to the store, he edged over to the gun counter. Bob noticed and asked what he was looking at. "That forty-five and holster. I'm thinking its time I learned how to shoot a pistol."

Bob looked at him a moment then said, "Now David, you know there is a lot more to shooting a pistol than just pulling the trigger. Pistols can get a feller killed if he don't know how to use one properly."

"I know Pa, and I want to learn. If I had one and really knew how to use it, maybe Margret wouldn't have been shot and Bill wouldn't have had to confront three armed men. If not for Kathy, he could have been killed."

Bob reached in the counter and brought out the gun and holster, handing it to him. "Now Son, you will not wear that on the street until I know you are good enough to handle it. Other than a lot of practice, who are you going to get to help you? I've seen men draw their gun and be damn fast about it. I wouldn't think there is a fast gun in Chloride."

"Do you remember that time when U S Marshal Shorty Thompson got them two killers right here, out there in the street? Now that was fast and he killed um both with one shot each. That one already had his gun out and was bringing it up to shoot. Now I know I'll never be that fast, but I want to be fast enough to protect myself and whoever."

"There's a box of cartridges over there on that shelf."

* * * *

Dick, Jeff, Albert and Edgar sat on that mountain all afternoon, watching their back trail. Jeff built a supper fire and opened two cans of beans, pouring them into a pan. "Albert, want'a get a dab more wood and add more grounds to that coffee?"

"Yeah, but what are we gonna do about watering the horses? They ain't had a drop all day, well since morning."

Dick was leaned back against his saddle and had just opened that bottle of tequila. Why no one knew, he only drank a little beer once in awhile. "Come morning we'll be watching to see if that sheriff is just slow er quit the trail. If we don't see nobody we'll ride on back down to the river."

Albert looked over at him as he was putting the bottle back in saddlebags. "Damn Dick, that's ten miles er better."

"So! There shor's hell ain't no water up here. If nobody is still follering, we'll go to the river and water the horses and fill our canteens. I's thinking we'd ride over to Sliver City and circle back to the hideout from the west. No chance of being seen. Hell if we run across it, we'll just rob that Mesilla, Lordsburg stage. I hear ever now and again they haul money to that Lordsburg bank."

That got everyone's attention. Jeff looked up from the heated beans and asked, "How much you figgering they haul? I mean could it be a good dab?"

"Now how in the hell would I know that? We'll be riding that'a way anyhow, so we may's well get it while we can. Yeah, no matter how much it is." He reached for a plate of beans and a cup of coffee.

Albert got his coffee and a plate of beans and said, "Let's count what we got from Chloride."

Dick took the spoon from this mouth saying, "Yeah, after we finish eating."

After a bit, Dick emptied his saddlebags and started

counting money into four piles. "Three hundred and sixteen damn dollars! That shor's hell ain't enough to hang for! Next time Jeff, don't be so damn quick on pulling the trigger. Killing that teller was a damn bad thing to do."

"Yeah but what if he had been going for a gun? I didn't want to take the chance of one of us getting shot."

"Jeff, you had yore gun in yore hand, cocked! If you'd waited to see what he brought out of that drawer, you wouldn't ah shot him an we'd have a few more hundred dollars. Yeah an we wouldn't be looking at a rope if they ever catch us. Damn it he could have had a family!"

"They'll never catch us Dick. We're too damn smart for um. Don't you think? I mean hells bells we've been robbing for over seven months and there ain't nobody even got close enough for a gunfight."

"You'd better hope the hell nobody ever gets close enough for a gun fight! One or more of us could die. Why in the hell do you think I go to all the trouble of scouting out our escape route? I'll tell you why! It's so we can outrun posses."

"Damn I know that Dick! And it's worked ever time."

Morning came and breakfast was over. Not one thing was seen on their back trail. "Alright, let's mount up and head for the river, but ever body keep their eyes open. We don't want to ride into no trap."

At this same time, Sheriff Dobbs and his posse were headed back for Chloride. Sal saw how disappointed Dobbs looked and said, "Sheriff, no body could'a done no better. We done what we could."

"I know that Sal, but it's a damn shame robbing killer bastards got clean away without a one of um taking no lead. Them suckers shor had that robbery planned. I just hope they try it again one day and I'm ready. They gotta hang for shooting that teller and Margret. She was such a sweet, pretty little girl. I'd guess Seth is right broke up about it. You know, being his only child and his wife dying three years back."

"You gonna get out posters when we get back?"

"Yeah, best I do so ever lawman can be on the lookout for um. They'll mess up one of these days."

It took well over three hours getting down that mountain and to the Rio Grande. While the horses drank and rested, the boys stepped from their saddles and lay in the shade of large old Cotton Wood trees. Albert asked, "We gonna ride back into Las Cruces?"

Dick half screamed, "Hell no! That Chloride sheriff might'a had his self a talk with the local sheriff, if he came that far. We'll cross the river here and ride on into Mesilla and get a few more days worth of trail grub. Maybe we can nose around and find out if that west bound stage is carrying any money on its next trip."

They crossed the river and headed north. Edgar asked, "You think they'll get posters out on us?"

Dick thought that over for a minute before saying, "Yeah maggin they will, with Jeff shooting that teller and you shooting a little girl. The only reason posters ain't already out is cause we never killed nobody. Now ever lawman in the territory will be watching for us."

Around two in the afternoon, David asked his father if it would be alright if he rode out and checked on Margret. He also wanted to practice with his new .45.

"That'll be alright, but you be back here by five. The Lopez family is bringing in fifty mine shoring poles and I want you to be here when they unload um. Them mines won't take no crooked er split poles."

He went for his horse and slipped his rifle into the saddle scabbard. Mounting, he waited until the edge of town to kick the horse into a slow lope. He took the thong from the hammer of his forty-five, pulled it free of the holster and spun the cylinder to check the loads.

Just as he dropped it back in the holster, he met three men riding for town. They were the same three that caused the ruckus in Bill and Kathy's café.

As he rode on toward the farm and ranch, he turned his head looking at the riders as they loped along. He rolled them over in his mind and commented to himself he had never seen them before except in the café. "Horse, I shor hope they don't give Kathy an Bill no more trouble."

He rode into the yard looking all round, but didn't see Mister Thomas. Tying his horse at the hitch rail, he didn't knock, just walked on inside, but called out as he neared Margret's room.

"Come on in David, I was expecting you sooner."

"Pop had me pretty busy today and I have to be back before five. How are you feeling?"

"Stiff and sore, but I know it could have been much worse. Doctor Williams said I could get up for a couple hours a day, starting tomorrow. I was wondering if you might could come out and help me so Papa can go on about his work."

"I'd like that, what time?"

"Oh anytime before it gets too awful hot."

"Alright around ten-o-clock then, does yer pa come to the house for dinner?"

"Yes, he's only out plowing the field just south of the barn. How long can you stay now?"

"Just a few minutes, I want to start shooting my pistol. I'm gonna learn how to use it right well."

"If you think you must. I just wish you didn't have to."

He reached and held her hand a moment, then told her he would see her at ten in the morning. Getting his horse he rode about a mile back toward town and dismounted. Tying the horse, he walked out ten feet or so and drew the pistol.

Looking around he saw a huge dead tree stump. Only half aiming, he pulled the trigger and saw he missed the stump by several yards. Gripping the butt tighter, he aimed better and only missed it by six or eight feet.

Lifting it where he could see down the sights, he pulled the trigger, but the smoke was so thick he couldn't tell if he hit the stump or not.

"Darn!" Holding it at arms length, he tried again but the shot went two feet high. In a huff, he shoved the gun into the holster, mounted and went on to town.

Riding straight to the livery and blacksmith's, he dismounted and called out to his friend. "Leo, are you in there?"

A young husky fellow of about nineteen years walked out. "Yeah I'm here, where'd you think I'd be?" Leo could tell there was something on his friend's mind.

"Leo, have you ever shot a pistol, much?"

"Yeah some, more'n a few times and got where I could hit the side of a barn with the doors and windows closed... Wait a minute! What'er you doing wearing one?"

"I wanted to get good enough to protect myself and anybody else. You know most ever body wears one."

"Yeah but most fellers growed up using one. It'd take a feller a long time to be any good, I'm thinking. Heck fire, yer gooder'n anybody about with yore rifle, just carry it."

"Yeah but most times I'd be needing my hands free."

Leo thought a minute then smiled, more to himself. "I think I can come up with something. How about loaning me yore rifle fer a week er so?"

"A week er so! What the heck for?"

"You'll see, you'll see. If you need one in the mean time, y'all got more."

David reached to his scabbard for the rifle and just as he was handing it to Leo, he glanced up the street. Leo looked that way to see what he was looking at. One man was being carried and two more were being helped by two men each toward the doctor's office.

"Darn, wonder what happened to them fellers, looks bad. I'd best get on over to the store, Paw might need me. Oh, do you mind taking care of my horse?"

"Go ahead, I got em."

David walked into the store and asked his father if he knew what had gone on that three men had to be helped to the doctor. His father looked up saying, "Naw might be some miners was hurt. Them poles should be here after a bit. Don't get off somewhere I can't find you."

"I'm just gonna go over to Kathy's and Bill's for a glass of ice tea. Want me to bring you back some?"

"Yeah, that'd be nice."

He walked into the café and sit down just as Kathy came walking out of the kitchen. "Oh David, I didn't hear you come in. What can I get you?"

"A big ol' glass of your ice tea. And when I'm done I'll be wanting to take one over to Pa."

As Kathy poured his tea, he looked around and asked, "Where's Bill"

"Here you go." She put the tea in front of him. "He had to…" Bill and six men walked in the front door talking.

The men picked out a table and sit down, as Bill walked on in the kitchen and washed his hands. David heard the men talking as one said, "I don't know for sure, but I don't think that one feller will ever use that gun arm again."

Another fellow added, "Yeah, I don't even know if the doc can save it er not, looks bad, looks bout blowed off."

Dub Jenkins was an old cowboy that just happened to be in the café, and had helped carry and drag the men to the doctor. He looked up and hollered out, "Kathy, where in the world is our coffee!"

"Hold yore horses Dub, I'm coming! I don't have but two hands!" As Bill started past, she handed him two cups of coffee. "Take one of these to Dub before he goes an bust a gut and you have to clean up the mess."

As the men got their coffee, David looked at the clock on the wall and stood. "I'll take Pop's ice tea now."

Kathy filled a glass about half full of ice then filled it with tea. "That'll be a dime, David."

He reached in his pocket for the dime and asked, "What all are they talking about?"

Kathy looked up, as if he should already know. "You know those three men that caused that ruckus in here?"

"Yeah."

"Well about an hour ago me an Bill was in the kitchen when Maggie, that's Bill's donkey. Well she started raising cane, so I looked out the window and there was them same three fellers with a rope around her neck.

"Bill grabbed my shotgun and lit out that door like his pants was on fire. He hollered at um and one stupid idiot went for his gun. Bill was too far away to kill um, but he shor put the hurt on um something fierce. Cedric will take um all to jail when Doc Williams get's um patched up. It'll be up to the sheriff what he does with um when he gets back."

CHAPTER THREE

While Dick and Albert got more trail grub from the grocery store and filled all canteens with water, Jeff and Edgar walked into the stage depot and asked when the next stage was pulling out for Lordsburg.

"That'd be six-o-clock in the morning sharp, y'all wanting a ticket? There'll be plenty of room as no one else has bought a ticket."

"Yeah we might, but I went an heard that stage sometimes carries money er gold. Now we don't want to be on no stage when it's robbed."

"Well it will be carrying money, but I'll have you know no stage on that run has ever been robbed."

"Wonder why that is?"

"I don't know, maybe because after you leave this valley, anybody could be seen coming for miles. That's mostly flat desert out there, most of the way. Got a stage stop where the horses are watered out about thirty miles and another in that little spot of Deming. We'll only have another month then the train will take the passengers and mail."

"Why don't the train just take it now?"

"Our contract with the Government won't be up till the first of May."

"You think maybe it would be safer for us just to take the train?" Jeff looked over at Edgar and winked where the man didn't see him.

"Naw no safer, but it'd be a whole lot faster. Course it cost more to ride the train. Yeah, higher than a cat's back."

Jeff grinned saying, "Thanks, we'll take the train, at least some outlaw wouldn't try stopping it."

The old man got about half huffy. "Ain't no outlaw

going to stop that stage either! You boys are just cowards."

They got their horses and met Dick and Albert on the west end of town. After telling of what the station master said, they all had a good laugh and headed west. "We'll beat that stage to the stage stop an hit it there, not out in the open."

Jeff acted as if he had ants in his pants. "I'd bet they'll be hauling a gob, don't you? Yeah a lot of money."

"We'll find out around nine-o-clock in the morning, now come on we've gotta cover some ground fore stopping for the night."

"Think there's any need to check out our escape route like we always do?"

Dick thought a minute before saying, "Naw, hell it's all wide open desert. We ride out like we's headed for Mexico, then middle afternoon we'll split up an ride west a good half day before turning north toward Silver City."

Edgar asked, "You mean we're gonna ride nine er so hours south before we turn around and go where we was gonna go to start with?"

"Well yeah, we gotta throw anybody off our trail."

"What er we gonna do for water for these horses?"

"Damn!" Dick thought a minute then said, "We'll buy four more canteens at the stage stop. One canteen apiece should hold the horses till we come across some."

"Uh, what if they don't got no canteens for sale?"

"Damn it I don't know! We'll think of something!"

They were only around five miles from the stage stop when they stopped for the night. "Edgar, you an Jeff hobble them horses right good. That's a thunder storm coming this'a way and it'll rattle um somewhat."

"Albert, help me tie these tarps to them mesquite trees. Maybe we'll stay a bit dry. No matter we'll get our asses wet fore this if over." Dick grabbed tarps from behind saddles and started tying them to mesquite trees.

"Jeff, you get done with them hobbles, grab up some of that dead mesquite for a fire. We want'a be done eating for it showers. Oh an get enough for morning coffee."

Just before dark they were through eating and the rain came. It wasn't a little shower that normally hit this desert it was a down pour of rain and small pea sized hail. The horses started raising hell and even in the rain and hail, Dick went out to calm them. When he got back under the traps he was dripping wet.

"They gonna be alright?" Albert knew horses' hated hail and most times ran their asses off when out in it.

"Yeah, I rope tied um to a big ol' mesquite."

It rained for over an hour and a half before slacking off as the storm moved toward the northeast. Dick laughed, "Well we won't have to worry about water for the horses. Ever low spot will be full for days."

The next morning the stage pulled out of Mesilla right at six-o-clock. Dick and the boys were having coffee and breakfast. After picking up camp, they headed off toward the stage stop in a slow lope.

Riding up in the yard, the station man called out from the barn, "Y'all go ahead and water yore horses. I'll be out in a minute, soon's I drop in a dab more feed to these horses."

The boys had dismounted while the horses lowered their muzzles in the horse trough. They all walked to the pump and refilled their canteens.

As the old man walked out Jeff asked, "Bout what time does the stage get in here?"

The old man pulled his dollar watch from his pocket, and squinted his eyes to look at the dial saying, "Less than a hour an ah half, they'll be here. Y'all boys want something while you wait? I mean if yer waiting."

"Yeah, if you got um I'd take a box of them sulfur matches and a couple of canteens."

"Don't got no canteens, but got the matches."

The old man walked on inside as the boys tied their horses at a hitch rail that was about to fall down. "Damn, hope these horses don't get spooked, they'd drag this damn thing plumb to Mexico."

Dick smiled, "We ain't gonna be here that long." They walked on inside and the man handed Dick the matches. "That's gonna be a nickel, want anything else? I just got in a case of them canned peaches, shor are nice."

"Yeah, by dogged yeah them sound right good. I'll take four cans, how much are they?"

"I know its mighty high, but they'll run you eight cents a can. Things just keep getting higher. Don't know how people will be able to eat fore too awful long."

Dick paid for everything and asked, "Does the stage driver an guard come in while the horses are drinking?"

"Yeah most times less they're running late then they don't. Don't run late all that often."

"Do many people ride the stage now a days?"

"Naw, not since that train came through. Looks like I'll be out of a job come May first." He laughed, "Maybe I'll just get me a job with the railroad."

After a bit they heard the stage coming, so the old man walked out to pump water. The boys stayed inside until the stage came to a jerking stop in the yard. They heard the old man holler out howdy and got one in return.

Dick looked through the window and nodded to the other three boys. "Jeff, when that driver and guard walk in, you go out and hold that old man, and damn it don't you kill him! We'll turn all the horses loose so no body can chase us."

The guard and driver walked in and over to the coffee pot. As they talked and filled their cups, three pistols were drawn, cocked and ready to shoot. "What is this?"

"Take it easy and nobody will get shot. Edgar, you and

34

Jeff bring in that old man, then unhook those horses and kick um and the ones in the corral loose."

"Wait a minute! You can't do that! We gotta get on to Lordsburg." The driver stepped forward and got a gun shoved in his belly."

"Mister, I'll blow yore belly button plumb through yore back bone! Now set yore ass down and keep shut!"

The old man was brought in then Jeff and Edgar headed back out to un-hitch the stage horses and turn the ones in the corral loose. Fifteen minutes later, they walked back inside carrying a small chest. Dropping it to the floor, Jeff shot the lock off and laughed as he swung open the lid. "Royal Flush! Damn we got it this time."

Dick never took his eyes off the men. "Get on the horses and bring mine right to the door. We'll be in Mexico before they can get any help." He looked the men in the eyes, "Now fellers, you don't go poking yore heads out that door before we ride off. One look and a rifle slug will make you change yore minds.

"Jeff, which way'd you run them horses?"

"Back east toward Mesilla."

"Good, you fellers might have thirty miles er so rounding up horses." They eased out the door, mounted and rode south in an all out run. After a few hundred yards, they pulled the horses back to a long easy lope.

The stage driver was busy filling two canteens. "You stay right here. If I can catch one of them horses maybe I can catch um all. If not it'll take me about five hours walking back to Mesilla. No matter, I'll be back."

He hung the canteen straps over his shoulders and started east at a fast walk, talking to himself. *"Damn, wouldn't you know, their headed for Mexico. Them little shits will never be caught. Turning my horses loose, dad gum it no way."*

After riding about two or three miles, the four boys

split up, riding in all directions. Before nightfall they would meet north along a low ridge of hills. Ever who got there first was to have a fire built and coffee on. That would be about thirty miles north, northwest of that stage stop.

The stage driver had no luck in catching the horses. He had followed tracks until they wondered off the road headed southeast. Staying to the road, he was about six miles west of Mesilla when two cowboys riding along looking for strays saw a man walking down the road.

Kicking their horses into a lope, they pulled up a few feet away from Gus. "Gus, what in the hell happened to yore stage?"

After talking a bit and taking a long drink from his canteen, he was helped up behind the saddle. "It's coming on night we'll take you on in. That's still a hell of a long walk." He thought a minute, "Wait a minute. Jeet, you'd better ride back to headquarters an let um know what I'm doing. Wouldn't want a bunch of the boys coming looking fer us. Tell um I'll be back fore mid-morning."

"Then you'll stay the night in Mesilla?"

"Hell yes, you don't think I'd ride back tonight, do you?"

"Naw, don't guess so." They split up with Jeet riding most too due south and Harley taking Gus on toward Mesilla.

"Harley, you don't know how glad I was to see you boys riding up. I don't think I could have made another few hours. I was give just about plumb out. I thought it'd only take five er so hours, but I've already been six."

"Yeah, walking shor ain't no fun."

The boys were eating supper and drinking coffee. Dick handed his cup to Edgar for one more cup full saying, "We may's well count what money we got out'a that box."

Ten minutes later they were laughing and talking like school boys. "Damn, thirty-two hundred dollars! That was a better haul than that damn bank an we didn't have to shoot no body. Now when we get close to Silver City, we'll split up again and ride in, in pairs. That way no body can say they ever saw four riders coming in at once."

Albert leaned back against his saddle saying, "You know Dick, I like the way we always split the money after a job. That'a way if one or two of us is caught, the others have money and can get away."

"Yeah but you'd better hope the hell none of us do get caught. It's hanging now, no prison."

They cleared camp about an hour after Gus headed back to the stage stop with a team of horses. The sheriff had been notified and told the outlaws had headed for Mexico.

Edgar looked over at Dick and asked, "Bout how long you thinking it'll take getting to Silver City?"

"Two days, less we see somebody on our back trail."

* * * *

David had gone out and visited with Margret everyday. As he rode back to the livery, he remembered his rifle. "I'd bet its ready by now."

It wasn't, the only thing Leo said was it was coming along. David unsaddled the horse asking what was taking so long. "Darn David, I've got other work to do. I only get to work on it at night after supper. Don't go getting a horse hair up yore butt. You'll like it when I'm done."

Two days later, after splitting up, Dick and the boys met at the Copper Dome Saloon. They had gotten into town three hours apart, and acted if they hadn't see each other in months. As they sat for a few games of poker, they talked loud enough for other people to hear what was said.

Dick got another beer asking, "Y'all still work on that ranch over north of here?"

"Yeah, took a few days off and come to town for a woman. Ain't had one yet but I will fore I leave."

It was mid-night before they had enough drinking and poker and got rooms right upstairs. Jeff and Edgar got a woman, but knew to keep their mouths shut around any whore. They'd talk their tongues off. One woman got to asking question of how come little cowboys had so much money to spend.

Jeff told her they hadn't been to town in a whole year. This was like Christmas and birthdays all rolled into one. She smiled, "Then you won't be coming back anytime soon?"

"Naw too damn far, but when I do come back I'll be shor an look you up."

"Thanks, but I won't be here."

"Yeah, why not?"

"I'm getting married next week. A nice boy what works for the Santa Rita Copper Mine asked me to marry him."

"Well I'll be dogged, I'm right happy for you."

Leaving Silver City after breakfast the next morning, it took two days getting to their hideout. Five miles away, they had split up again, leaving only one set of tracks going in every direction. Dick got to the old mine first and went about taking care of his horse.

As the others rode up and dismounted, he took his horse into the pole corral and saw fresh horseshit. "Hey fellers!"

Jeff was closest and asked, "Yeah, what?"

"We've had company, fresh horse shit right here."

Everyone quickly looked around with Edgar asking, "Think it was the law?"

"Now how in the hell would I know that? Ever who it was stayed overnight. Looks like one man had two horses cause there is only one set of boot tracks, and there are three more piles of horseshit right over there close. Albert, go in and see if any of our stuff is missing. I'm gonna foller these tracks out yonder a ways. Come on Jeff, you come too. Oh,

Edgar, while we do that, you go ahead and take our saddle-bags an what food we have on in and stack it up."

They followed tracks for several hundred yards, but they were not headed toward Chloride, they were going northwest. Jeff asked, "What do you make of it, Dick?"

"Not sure, might have just been somebody that stumbled onto this place and it was coming on night, so he just stayed. We'll have to keep our eyes open from now on."

Jeff was worried because this was the first time anyone had found their hideout. "Dick, why don't I get my horse and track em just to make sure he ain't going after nobody an coming back. We could be caught off guard."

"Yeah, that might not be a bad idea. Just don't go getting yore ass in a crack. If he is going to Milligan's Plaza, you won't be back fore four er five days."

"Yeah, but I gotta know. I just don't want him turning back toward Chloride. By them tracks he's just walking the horses. I might catch up fore too awful long." He saddled his horse and took up the trail just as the other boys walked from the mine. Edgar asked where Jeff was going.

"Follering them tracks to make sure that feller ain't coming back and bring somebody along with him. Anything of ours missing?"

"No nary a thing. Looks like he just eat and slept is all."

They all stood outside looking off in the distance. Albert shifted from one foot to the other saying, "I'm thinking we might ought'a be looking for us another of these old abandon mines, and move fore something does happen."

Dick nodded his head up and down. "Yeah we could do that, there's plenty of um around here. Some of um ought'a have corrals for the horses. When Jeff gets back we just might do that. You know, a couple of us at a time, leaving two here to watch after things."

Late that evening, just before sundown, Jeff saw

smoke from a campfire. Riding in slow, he saw it was in a large clearing with one man eating supper. He was going to dismount back in the timber and go the rest of the way on foot, but one of the man's horses raised his head and gave out with a long whinny.

"Crap! Oh well I'll ride in easy." He removed the thong from the hammer of his pistol and rode on. Getting close enough to where he figured the man could hear, he called out, "Hello the fire! Can I ride in?"

"Yeah, plenty of room."

He rode up and dismounted, as he did the man said, "You got a cup, I've got coffee."

"Thanks, I could sure use a dab of hot coffee." Reaching into his saddlebags, he said over his shoulder, "Jeff Barnes." He sure wasn't going to say Jeff Nibbs.

"Howdy Jeff, Clinton Naylor."

Clinton reached and poured Jeff his coffee. "Got a bite of beans left here if you care for some."

"Yeah, if you was gonna throw um out, I'll eat um."

They talked and drank coffee and after a bit Clinton got around to asking, "What in the world are you doing riding around on these mountains and in tall timber?"

"Headed over to Kingston fer a spell."

"Kingston? Never heard of it, where's it at?"

"South of here fifty er so miles."

"South, what'er you doing riding north?"

"Come across yore tracks and thought I'd see who it was. I know a bunch of cowboys what ride through here now and again. Where are you headed?"

"On north about what I figger to be a hundred miles yet to go. Thought I's taking a short cut, but you see how that turned out."

"Damn, I've been around here a good while and ain't heard of a town a hundred miles north of here, cept Magdalena an Kelly."

"Naw it ain't a town. I got me a punching job on the B Bar S Ranch. I do guess it's a good bit more west and north."

"The B Bar S, don't a U S Marshal own that place?"

"I wouldn't know that. I got a letter from a feller name of Buffalo Blackburn saying he needed punchers. Hell he pays forty a month, an you can't beat that."

"Then you'd not be from around Chloride?"

"Naw rode through there though. That looks to be a nice little mining town, shor busy."

"If you rode through Chloride what'er you doing coming from the south? Chloride is damn near due east."

"Yeah, I got turned around and rode upon that big assed mountain right over yonder. Last night I come across what looked like a mine to me, but nobody was around so I just spent the night. Hell there was a damn good corral for my horses. Looked like nobody had been there in a good while. I guess they didn't hit nothing, so they upped an pulled out."

They talked until rolling in their bedrolls for some sleep. The next morning after coffee, they went different ways. Jeff would be glad to get back and tell the boys they had nothing to worry about.

CHAPTER FOUR

The morning was slow and David was sweeping the front walkway when the sheriff and his posse came riding in. David leaned the broom against the wall and walked down to the sheriff's office.

They had all dismounted, with two of the fellows taking the horses toward the livery. Sheriff Dobbs had just dropped down in his chair as David walked in. "Howdy Sheriff, I see you didn't catch nobody."

"Naw, follered um plumb to Mesilla and figger there was no need in us going on to El Paso. Figger they're in Mexico by now."

"Yeah, well it's a cinch they ain't from no where around here er somebody would'a remembered seeing um."

Dobbs opened a desk drawer and got out a piece of paper. "David, can you draw any?"

"Well yeah a little bit, why?"

"Think you could draw up some pictures of them fellers so I can get um sent around to all the law?"

"Yeah I could, but Margret would be a lot better at that than me."

"I meant to ask, how's she doing?"

"Better ever day, she gets up and walks out on the porch and sets and reads."

"Do you think you could take the time to go out an see if she would draw us up some pictures?"

"Yeah, I was gonna go out and visit with her around one anyway. I have to be back around three. Some freighters are bringing in a load for the store an I have to check it in."

David headed back to the store, but turned for the

42

livery. He wanted to see if his rifle was ready. "Howdy Leo, how's my rifle coming?"

A broad grin covered Leo's face. "Come on, I want to know what you think about it."

They walked over to the tack room and Leo reached right inside the door. He handed a little sawed of looking something to David. "Well?"

"Leo, what in the hell did you do to my rifle?"

"Cut off the barrel an stock, making it fourteen inches long and made the trigger guard three inches round."

"I can see that, but why in the world would you do it?"

Leo started to frown, but smiled and said, "Come on out back an I'll show you. Oh wait." He reached back inside the tack room and brought out a weird looking something, smiling all the while he strapped it around his waist and tied a leather strap around his leg.

Davis watched as he took the sawed off rifle and clipped it in that thing and headed for the back door. Once out back, he shoved a couple cartridges into the rifle and clipped it back to his leg. Smiling he said, "Now watch this."

With his right hand he grabbed the rifle, bringing it up as his left hand grabbed the top of the barrel. Jacking in a cartridge and pulling the trigger, a split second later the other cartridge was fired. He hit his target both times."

David was surprised at the speed and just how accurate he was. Leo was smiling so big it got David to smiling. "Now David, I'm figgering you practice with this a little while an there won't no body be able to out draw you with no pistol. And it shor's hell shoots straighter."

"How in the world did you come up with this idea? Yeah and even making a holster with no front to hold it."

"Now that was the hard part, oh an filing the rifles in the barrel after I cut it off. But you can see the rifling is working just the way it's supposed to. Yeah an look at this."

He unbuckled it from his waist and the strap from his leg, showing David two leather covered metal clips.

"Now I made these clips out'a that heavy barn roof metal. I cut it down and used the forge to heat and shape um the way I wanted to. Then I used the heaviest bull hide I had laying around here. No body can see nothing but leather and that sawed off rifle. What do you think?"

"I think you must be crazy, but I've never seen anything like it. Now I see what was taking you so dad gummed long. Heck yeah, I won't have to learn how to use a pistol after all. I can't wait to get out yonder and get use to it."

"Now you know I'm fair when it comes to using a pistol. Why don't you come around close to sundown an we'll go out to that ol' mine slag pile an do some shooting."

"Yeah, I'd like that. Well I'd best get back over to the store. I'm riding out to see Margret around one."

He started to walk off but Leo quickly said, "Oh darn! I damn near forgot the most important thing."

"Yeah, what's that?"

"You have to be darned careful with that rifle. You don't have to pull the trigger less you want to."

"What?"

"Yeah, when you jack another cartridge into the firing chamber and bring that trigger guard up right fast, it hits a pin that releases the hammer and fires the gun without pulling the trigger. Here, let me show you."

With no cartridge in the rifle, Leo slowly showed him and they both heard the firing pin fall when the trigger guard was pulled up after a cartridge would have gone into the firing chamber. "Good Lord, no wonder you fired that last shot as fast as you did."

"Yeah, you've gotta be careful if there is a cartridge in the chamber. You'll blow yore leg off er kill somebody you didn't want to."

"Now I know what you meant when you said only a

few fast guns could beat me. Thanks Leo, if this really works and it looks like it will, why don't you get in touch with the Winchester Fire Arms Company an show um your idea?"

"Naw, I'm thinking every outlaw would get one. Then a whole lots of folks would be in trouble."

"Yeah, guess yer right. I'll see you this evening."

David went back to the store and told his father the sheriff wanted he and Margret to draw up posters. "Best you go on an do that. It's mighty important them drawings get out as soon as possible."

An hour later Margret had one drawing done and was working on another when her father came in to eat dinner. Margret looked up saying, "Oh my God! Papa I am so sorry, I should have had your dinner ready. We just got busy drawing up posters on those killers and robbers."

"Slow down Honey, I've fixed our meals for a month. A few more times won't hurt me."

She looked at him with almost a blank stare. "Why did that slip my mind? It's as though for the time I forgot I'd been shot. Well we all know I am much better and Doctor Williams said I could start doing my normal chores by weeks end."

"Honey stop worrying about it and go right on with what you are doing. I have a beef roast here and will just cut myself off a slab of that and get on back out to the field."

The drawings took much longer than David thought it would. By the time they were finished the hour was late and the sun was no more than an hour and a half in the western sky. He had not made it back to town by three. "Thanks Margret, best I get but I'll be out tomorrow." He squeezed her hand just as her father stepped through the door.

"I see yer still here, David."

"Yes Sir, we just finished and I was just about to leave. Sheriff Dobbs wants to get these over to the newspaper office where they can run off a bunch of copies."

"Let me take a look at them."

David handed him the drawings and watched his face. "My Lord, these look like some of them pictures. Any body that sees these shor won't miss them boys if they show their faces in some town. Did the Sheriff say how many he was having printed up?"

"Naw, just said he wanted them on the morning stage. Said they'd go to every post office an sheriff's office in the whole territory. One of the deputies will nail a gob of um up right around town."

David got his horse and took him to the water trough for a drink before riding into town. As he tied up in front of the sheriff's office, he looked across and down the street to make sure Leo still had the livery open.

Sheriff Dobbs looked at the drawings saying, "This is a mighty fine job. Before I take them to the newspaper, I'm gonna stop by the bank and show um to Mister Aldan and see what he thinks. You and Margret did a mighty fine job."

"I've gotta go now. I'm to meet up with Leo and we're gonna go out to the slag pile and shoot."

As Sheriff Dobbs stood, he noticed the contraption strapped to David's right thigh. "What in the world is that?"

"It's my rifle, .44-40. Leo fixed it up for me."

"Looks like he ruined a good rifle to me."

Thirty minutes later, Leo and David were at the slag pile. "Here Leo, you shoot it a few times and let me watch."

Leo smiled as he strapped the holster to his leg. "Oh another thing I forgot to show you. Now watch my right hand at how I hit the stock just back of the hammer."

Leo popped the stock and it was as though the rifle jumped into his hand. "Darn! Let me see you do that again."

Several times Leo popped the stock, letting David see exactly how he did it. "Now what happens is it pops the barrel loose from the lower clip then you grab the barrel with your left hand, jack a cartridge into the firing chamber with your right hand and all within the blink of an eye."

They worked with the rifle until after sundown and both knew they must get back to town. David was very impressed and knew with lots of practice he could get very good. Leo already was, so David figured he had practiced a good bit while perfecting the clips.

As they rode back to town David said, "You know Leo, for making this for me, I'll give you a rifle and you can make one for yourself."

Leo smiled, "Yeah, one of these days I just might do that. Oh David, it'd be best if you told nobody where you got that. Well yer pa and Margret would be alright, I guess."

"Tell nobody! Why? Darn it looks as if you'd be proud letting people know what kind of work you can do."

"Naw then there'd be more fellers wanting one. I don't have the time. I just did that one for you cause we're right good friends."

"Thanks Leo and yes, we are very good friends. But what am I gonna tell people when they ask me where I got it? You know they're gonna ask."

"Then it'd be best if you told a little white lie an say you done it. Nobody is to know it was me, promise?"

"Yeah shor, I promise."

Spring was over and middle summer was here. The days were hot and even the miners were glad to be working underground. During the heat of the day in front of every store, people sat in chairs, fanning themselves.

David had practiced with his rifle until he was not only fast, but he hit a small target almost every time. He had that gun strapped to his leg from the time he left the house in the morning until supper time everyday.

The seventeenth of July, his father said he would have to take the wagon and go to Las Palomas for two windmills a rancher had ordered from Chicago. They were coming in by train. It looked to be another dry year and the rancher already had two wells dug, while waiting on the windmills. "Now Son, its two days there and a good two days back loaded. You shouldn't run into no trouble, but don't you take no chances. When you set up night camp, be sure you are well out in the open where you can see or hear anybody riding up."

"When do I leave?"

"Before sunup in the morning. I've got all of your food and coffee ready. You'll just need your bedroll, tarp and raincoat. When we harness the horses in the morning, I'll have Leo throw on fifty pounds of grain. Oh shoot, I just thought of something. You might can stay at the stage stop. You'll have to stop there anyhow to water the horses."

"Will it be alright if I ride out right quick and tell Margret how long I'll be gone? I wouldn't want her worrying cause of not coming around."

"Sure go on, but be back for supper."

By the time the sun broke the horizon, David was several miles down the road toward Las Palomas. Over west seventy or so miles, Dick was in the lead as the four boys made their way to Alma.

Jeff was wanting to hit the small bank saying the town didn't even have a sheriff. Before getting to town, they split up and rode into town from the south and north. Each pair rode from one end of town to the other then stopped in front of the bank, all at the same time.

Albert stood with the horses, digging at an unseen object in his horse's hoof. Dick, Jeff and Edgar walked inside and saw only one customer, the banker and one teller.

The customer didn't leave when finished at the teller cage, but walked around to the banker's desk. "Mister Thornton, here's the last twenty dollars I owe you. You know what kind of a bind you pulled me out of by loaning me…"

"Hands up! Anybody grab for a gun an yer all dead!"

Jeff was already behind the teller's cage with a gun in the man's face. Edgar quickly covered the customer and banker. Dick walked over, grabbing the banker by the arm. "Load that money from that safe in these saddlebags!"

Thornton was scared to death. He had never been robbed and this could ruin this small town. "Mister, please don't do this. This is all the money this town has, it will ruin us. We don't have all that much to start with."

With the robbery over, the four boys rode north toward Milligan's Plaza. After a few miles they rode west until coming to the San Francisco River. There they turned northeast, riding in the water.

They rode past the road ten miles north of Alma. After a few hundred yards they cut east by southeast. Jeff smiled, "What'd I tell you, no law."

"Yeah but it'll be a good while fore we can ride back this'a way. We're gonna have to start going farther and farther away from the hideout to hit any bank."

Albert just thought of something. "Why don't we find us a second hideout? I know there's gotta be a few abandon mines west of Kingston and maybe around Hillsboro."

Dick looked over at him as they rode slowly up the mountain. "Now that ain't a bad idea. Day after tomorrow we'll just ride down that'a way and take a look."

Jeff cracked a smile saying, "Yeah, and as we go we can stop through Chloride and get all of that bank's money."

Dick didn't stop but said over his shoulder, "Now hold on. We could be recognized just riding down the street. Naw I don't think four months is near long enough to stay out'a a town. That town will remember us a long time being as we left two people dead."

"I was just thinking being as we might be pulling out, we ought'a hit it one more time and clean out that safe."

"Well I'm for leaving it alone until fall then hit it. If this winter is as bad as last, we won't be doing much robbing anyway." Dick thought a minute longer then said, "I'll tell y'all what we'll do. When we head out to Kingston, we'll ride through Chloride one at a time, fifteen minutes apart. We'll meet half way to Winston where we'll cut south. Now I don't want nobody stopping in town for nothing, nor talking to nobody. Just ride through with your eyes open.

"We'll meet around that curve southeast of town and don't nobody even think of riding into Winston."

They made the hideout right at dark. Jeff and Edgar took care of the horses while Dick and Albert went on inside and built a fire. With coffee water on heating they opened two cans of beans and a sack of hardtacks.

As saddles were leaned against the fence Jeff looked around and said, "Now Edgar, I'm thinking me an you can rob that bank. We'll let Dick an Albert ride on ahead and we'll bring up the rear."

"You really think just you an me can pull it off?"

"Heck yeah, it'll just be that banker and he might not even have his self a new teller. We won't shoot nobody just bust their skulls with our gun butts. We'll be plumb gone fore anybody even knows it happened."

"Alright, but what will Dick say when he finds out what we went an done?"

"Smile as we split all that money."

The next morning after breakfast and coffee, they started making sure nothing would be left that could tie this place into them. Albert asked, "You mean we won't be coming back here?"

"We might, but if we can find a better place even closer to banks and the stage line, it'll be awhile fore we're back."

They saddled the horses and looked around one more time before riding off. A mile west of town, Dick and Albert started on with Albert dropping back well before getting to town. Jeff and Edgar checked their guns, making sure the cylinders were full.

They gave Dick and Albert about thirty minutes then rode slowly into town, looking all around. Pulling up in front of the bank, they stayed mounted while looking up the street toward the sheriff's office.

Stepping from the saddles Jeff commented, "Looks kind'a quiet this morning." Dropping the reins over the hitch rail, but not tying them they walked inside.

Not one customer was in the bank, so Edgar walked around behind the teller's cage with his gun in his hand. Mister Aldan was going over papers at his desk and hadn't heard them walk in.

As Jeff cocked his pistol and shoved in right into the banker's face, Mister Aldan jerked back with a start. "Remember me, banker Man? Load that money in these saddlebags, now!"

Mister Aldan recognized this boy as the one that shot Lee. He stood, took the saddlebags and kneeled in front of the safe. Jeff kept his pistol touching the back of his head. In less than three minutes, they walked out with full saddlebags.

Just at they mounted and turned their horses, Mister Aldan rushed to the door firing his pistol. The horses raced off with Edgar taking a slug in his lower back. He screamed and grabbed the saddle horn with his left hand.

Jeff slowed to ride beside him. "How bad are you hit?"

"Don't know, but feels bad. I can feel blood running inside. I can hold on, but I don't know for how long."

"Hang on we'll make it to Dick an Albert. Dick'll know what to do."

Less then twenty minutes later, they saw Dick and Albert waiting among tall trees. Dick saw Edgar riding slumped over in the saddle. "Albert, trouble coming, get ready to ride. There'll be a posse along after a bit."

Jeff pulled up a few feet away with a worried look. "Dick, me an Edgar hit that bank and as we was riding off that damn ol' man shot Edgar. What'er we gonna do?"

"We've gotta split up. Looks like Edgar can't hold out with these horses in a dead run. You stay with him and go on to the creek at a southeast angle. Once in the water, turn back west and stay in the water as long as you can. Get him on back to the hideout. Heat water and clean that wound as soon as you get there.

"You've still got well over half a bottle of that tequila, so pour on a dab of that and give him a swallow er two. Me an Albert will let the posse see us then we'll out run um. It might be a day er two, but we'll see you at the hideout."

Dick and Albert rode back north toward the Chloride, Winston road. "Now Albert, you know Jeff went and got us in a real bind. We'll let the posse see us from a good ways off then high tail it to the Rio Grande. If we have to split up, I'll meet you in Socorro two days from now at the Owl Saloon."

"I'm worried this time Dick, real worried."

"Yeah me too. Jeff just got us into more trouble."

They stayed in their saddle right in the middle of the road. From this low rise they could see a good half mile back toward Chloride. After a good half hour, Dick was ready to ride on when around a bend rode seven riders, dust boiling up behind their horses.

"Posse, I hope they see us before…" At that moment a slug tore off a rock with a deadly whine. "Damn, come on! One of them bastards has a Sharps' er Henry!"

They had their horses at top speed in only a few jumps. Down the east side of the rise they went and out of sight of the fast moving Posse. Twenty minutes later they rode through Winston without slowing.

Albert hollered over to Dick, "We heading on into Las Palomas?"

"Naw, we'll cut straight east at Monticello and make the river. If it's not too high I want to cross over to the east side. There's less arroyos coming down toward the river from that side. How's yore hoss holding out?"

"Damn good, yours?"

"Yeah, we'll make it. That Posse had already run their horses four er five miles so they'll be give plumb out by now."

Sure enough Sheriff Dobbs had pulled his posse back to where the horses were only in a long ground eating lope. As they rode into Winston, they brought their horses to a dusty stop in front of the first man they saw.

He shouted, "Sheriff Dobbs from Chloride! Did a couple of fellers come through here a short bit ago?"

"Yep shor did an busting ass they was. Never even slowed one bit. I guess y'all'ud be after um?"

Dobbs and the posse were already pushing their horses down the street and out of town. The man riding closest to Dobbs called out, "Think they'll head fer Mexico this time?"

"Might, but if they are by damned they won't make it. I'll be waiting in Las Cruces."

"Bull crap! How'er you gonna do that?"

"When I see that's the way they're going, I'll take the train an beat um there. I'll get the sheriff an we'll lay a trap out north of town."

Within just a few miles, Albert asked why they stayed with the stage road toward Cuchillo instead of riding across country to Monticello.

They had pulled the horses back to a steady lope as Dick called back. "That's rough country and now is not the time to lame a horse. We'll stay the stage road to where it gets close to the river an meets the one from the north. There we'll go on down to the river."

It was well after sundown and pushing dark by the time they rode down the south bound stage road. They let the horses walk a few hundred yards then one at a time left the road and cut east toward the river. "If that river ain't too awful high, we'll cross over and make camp. I'm most to sure that posse has already stopped when they couldn't see tracks."

"We gonna build us a fire? I shor am needing beans an coffee. We ain't eat nothing but jerky since breakfast."

"Yeah, if we can find a spot where it won't be see from the west. That ought'a be easy as them trees are pretty thick and there a few sand dunes over that'a way."

The water was breast deep on the horses and running pretty swift. They were pushed down stream much farther than they thought they would be. It was a good two hundred yards before the horses found bottom and pulled themselves up the east bank.

Riding on through trees and to where they thought a campfire wouldn't be seen, they dismounted. While Albert got wood and built a fire, Dick unsaddled and took care of the horses. In no time they were eating beans and drinking coffee.

"Dick, what do you think Jeff an Edgar are doing right about now?"

"I don't know, but Edgar was in mighty bad shape. I don't know if he'll even make it er not. If that slug ain't got out'a there he'll damn shor get lead poison an die."

"Think Jeff'ud know how to take out a bullet?"

"Hell no! He don't even know how to pick his own nose. If that slug went all the way through an Jeff keeps dropping a few drops of that tequila on the wound, he might have a chance. I just can't figger why in the world Jeff tried that bank after me telling not to even stop in town."

Jeff and Edgar made it back to the hideout without too much trouble. They stopped in front of the mine and Jeff helped Edgar from the saddle and took him inside. "You set right there an I'll get yore bedroll an saddle."

Jeff took care of the horses then fixed Edgar a better place to lie down. "I'll get coffee on, you hungry?"

"Yeah somewhat, but that coffee sounds damn good.

You gonna get water on to clean this wound?"

"Yeah, figgered to do that while we's drinking coffee."

CHAPTER FIVE

Somewhere well before midnight, Jeff was awakened by Edgar's groaning. "Yeah, yeah I'm awake. What'd yah need?"

"Water."

Jeff struck a sulfur match and lit a candle before lighting a lantern. Getting his canteen, he kneeled beside Edgar. "Here you go."

Edgar took the canteen in both hands and drank almost a third of it. Taking it from his mouth he asked, "Jeff, think you could dig this bullet out'a me?"

"Naw, you know I couldn't do nothing like that."

"Darn it if you don't I'm gonna die."

"I'll go bring the doc." He picked up his saddle and bridle then dropped it getting his canteen. Here is a full canteen I'll be back in less than four hours."

He grabbed up his saddle and headed for the corral. As fast as he could he threw on the bridle and saddle and headed out. He pushed the horse as hard as he could in this mountainous terrain and made Chloride in record time.

Now to find where the doctor lives. The only place he saw horses and heard people shouting and talking was the saloon. He stepped through the bat-wing doors and went straight to the bar. "Hey Mister, can you tell me where the doc lives? My mama needs him right bad."

"Sure son, four blocks up the street and two over. It's the big white house on the corner."

"Thanks." He turned and quickly got his horse and rode the six blocks. He jumped off his horse and rushed to the door. Knocking loudly, he waited a couple seconds then banged again.

He saw a lamp light and voice call out, "I'm coming! Hold your horses!" Doctor Williams opened the door, wearing his night cap and gown. "What do you need, Boy?"

"I need you to come with me, now. Get yore bag with stuff to remove a bullet. Do you have a horse?"

"Yes around back. Why, where are we going?"

"About twenty miles."

"Twenty miles! No, not this time of night. I'll go in the morning." He stood holding the lamp watching Jeff.

Jeff drew his gun and said, "You'll get some clothes on and come now, er I'll walk in there an kill yore wife and you can come wearing them night clothes! Now move!"

Jeff went inside while the doctor dressed and got his bag, making sure he had everything he would need. Going out the back door to the barn, Jeff helped saddle the horse then they went back around front for his.

After Jeff mounted, he took the doctor's handkerchief and blind-folded him. "You don't have to do that, Son."

"Yes I do if you want'a live. You can't see where we're going er you could come back with a posse."

Just under two hours later they pulled up at the mine. Jeff reached over and took the neckerchief off the doctor's eyes. "Get down."

Jeff took him inside where Edgar was asleep. "There he is doc. He's got a bullet in him."

Doctor Williams kneeled and looked Edgar over. "Do you have any more light?"

"Yes, two more lanterns."

"Then get them lit and water on."

As lanterns were lit and a fire built, Doctor Williams removed Edgar's shirt and looked the wound over. Within twenty minutes the water was hot and the doctor went to work. Edgar had come to and was told what was about to happen. Putting chloroform on a clean cloth, he held it over Edgar's face for about a minute.

Using alcohol, he kept bathing the wound and all around. After several minutes he said to himself, though Jeff heard him say, "I've got to cut that out."

Jeff jumped, "What? What er you gonna cut out?"

"I've got the slug, but there is a piece of hip bone buried in there. I can feel it but can't see it. I've got to get it out or later on it could cause him great pain and might even kill him, if it moved around any.

"Hold that lantern right over here. A bit more to your left, there, hold it right there." It took a couple of minutes but the doctor pulled a one inch sliver of bone from the bloody hole. It took another fifteen minutes cleaning and sewing up the hole before bandages were placed just at and below where his belt would ride.

As he finished and washed his hands, he was talking to Jeff. "Now Boy, that wound has to be cleaned twice a day and the bandages changed. If you can keep down the infection, he'll be alright and be able to ride in less than a month."

"Thanks Doc, you gonna leave them bandages an stuff I need?"

"Yes and the alcohol, you will need every bit of it. You be sure he eats and drinks plenty of water. Now can you take me back to town?"

"Naw, it'll be too light fore we got there, we'd better hold off till tonight. I don't want'a get shot."

"Now Son, I helped your friend here. I need to get on back as I have other people that need tending. Just blindfold me again and take me to where I'd know my way to town. You don't have to go all the way in with me."

"Yeah, I can do that. Come on."

Two and a half hours later they were on the road half way between Chloride and Winston. Jeff told him where they were and it was light enough for the doctor to see he was right. Reaching in his pocket, Jeff pulled out a ten dollar gold piece and handed it to the doctor. "Thanks Doc. That feller is more than a friend, he's my brother." He turned and rode off toward Winston and Doc Williams turned his horse west toward Chloride."

As the sun came up, Jeff was over half way back to the hideout. Doc was in bed asleep, getting some much needed rest. Sheriff Dobbs and his posse were a few miles north of Las Palomas, where they met David. Stopping to talk, David was told those same boys came back and robbed the bank.

"Did they shoot anybody this time?"

"No, but it looks like they might be headed back to Mexico. I am going to stop um this time."

"I didn't meet nobody on the road."

"I'd think they stayed the night in Las Palomas, or maybe went on and camped down by the river. Well we've gotta ride, I want to be on the morning train to Las Cruces."

Dick and Albert were ten miles north, riding the east side of the river, headed toward Socorro. They were riding east of the tree line and making pretty good time. Dick knew this close to the trees no one could see them from the west.

Neither boy had spoken more than a few words since morning coffee. Albert knew Dick had a lot on his mind. "What'er you thinking, Dick?"

"I'm thinking we've been doing a lot of wrong. Darn it I should have knowed sooner er later somebody was gonna get killed. You know I never wanted that. I just don't know what to do. I've got a lot of thinking and planning to do to make sure we don't get caught. It'll take a dab of time but I'll come up with something."

"Think maybe we ought'a just head fer home?"

"Naw if they ain't already, they'll be papers out on us an I wouldn't want Maw to worry none. We'll send her some money first chance we get."

"You really think papers on us would get that far east?"

"Might."

Paul L. Thompson

"Do you know where we're going yet?"

"Naw, just riding an thinking."

"What'll Jeff an Edgar do when we don't come back?"

"No idea, but it's a cinch us four can't ride together no more. They'll be looking for the four of us."

Jeff was back at the hideout and found Edgar awake but resting. He made coffee and they drank a couple cups, as Jeff told about the doc. "Now Edgar, I'm gonna sleep for a few hours. You need something, wake me."

Nightfall found Sheriff Dobbs and the Las Cruces sheriff camped twenty yards east of the road, north of town. "You thinking maybe they'll get here some time in the morning?"

"Naw, more like tomorrow evening late. If you've got things to do in town, you go ahead. I'll just set it out."

"Yeah but by you not bringing that posse with you, you could get yoreself in a bind."

"No need them coming, I just sent um on back to Chloride. My deputy might need help if anything else happened while I's gone."

Dick and Albert had pulled up at San Antonio, and ate supper in the café before riding down to the river to camp. After supper they were leaned back against their saddles and Dick said, "I think it'll be best if we load up with trail grub here an by-pass Socorro. If there's already papers out on us they'd for sure have um by now."

"How far north are you thinking we gotta ride?"

"Out of this territory is all I know. Maybe all the way to Colorado er even Wyoming. We go up there an get us a job way away from any town, we might have a chance."

"Yeah, I'm beginning to think we'd been better off if we'd stayed working for the Pitch Fork, instead of Jeff robbing that feller in town. If only we all hadn't run."

"Yeah but you know that ol' man's friend saw Jeff right good when he done it. If they'd caught him he'd got maybe

60

five years. Us being friends most of our lives, we had to try an help him get away. Course the way things have turned out, it might'a been best if he had been caught. Albert, we ain't ever again gonna let friends drag us into anything else. I mean if we don't get caught an hang."

"Think Jeff an Edgar will get caught?"

"No idea, but Edgar was shot up pretty good. If that bullet wadn't got out, he'll be dead in a couple more days."

"Why do you think Jeff went an robbed that bank? We didn't need the money."

"Just plain ol' hard headed, I reckon."

David had pulled into Chloride late in the evening. He just took the wagon load around back of the store and took the horses to the livery. It was too late today, but come early morning he'd ride out and let Margret know he is back.

After supper he and his dad were on the front porch when four men come riding up the street. Looking from side to side, as they past the front of the store they were over heard saying, "This don't look to be much of a town for Blake to be hiding in."

Another one said, "Dad blame it, this is where I was told he's at. Let's drop by the saloon an see if he's there."

At that very moment, Mister Sawyer stepped from the newspaper office, turned and locked the door. As he headed toward where Bob and David were, one of the men hollered out. "Blake! I told you, now yer a dead Man!"

Mister Sawyer hit the walkway on his belly, crawling and crabbing sideways for the alley. Shots were fired his way as a horse shied, David jumped up grabbing his rifle from his leg. He walked out into the street jacking cartridges into the firing chamber, knocking two men from their saddles.

The other two men turned their guns toward him and fired twice, but too late. David knocked them from their saddles with two shots. Rushing up, he saw nether was dead.

He shoved the rifle into one of their faces. Bob grabbed the other's gun and looked to see Mister Sawyer walking over.

"What was that all about, Blake?"

"When I had my paper in Santa Fe, I published their pictures right on the front page. They were demanding protection money from every business. When I did that they came after me. I slipped out the back door of my shop and got away, but my paper had already been sent all over the territory.

"U S Marshal Shorty Thompson caught up with them and Judge Carver gave them five years in prison. A year ago I got word they would be released within a month. Being as they said they would get me, I left Santa Fe and moved my paper down here. It took them all this time to find me."

Other men had walked up to see what all the shooting was about. One of them went for the deputy. Two men dead, two men needing a doctor and were walked to jail.

Mister Sawyer reached for David's hand. "David, I guess you know you saved my hide. They sure meant to kill me for sure this time."

"I'm just glad me an dad was out on the porch an heard um talk as they rode past."

"That was some mighty fancy shooting. May I see your rifle?" Blake held out his hand.

"Don't touch anything but the barrel an stock, it can go off without warning."

"Good Lord! What made you come up with something like this?"

"After the teller was killed an Margret shot, I knew I had to be able to do something if there was a next time. Yeah and I wadn't worth a hoot with a pistol."

As they talked, they saw Doctor Williams walking toward the jail. Blake reached and shook hands with Bob and David one more time, sincerely thanking them."

After breakfast and with the store opened, David went

to the livery for his horse. Leo was all smiles as he said, "I guess you showed them fellers, huh?"

"Yeah, guess so. I'm headed out to check on Margret and'll be back in a couple of hours. Oh, Blake wanted to know where I got my rifle."

"You didn't tell him!"

"Oh no, and I won't. Member, I promised."

"Good, him being a newspaper man he'd more'n likely smear it all over the front page."

David had a good visit with Margret and got back to town right at noon. As he tied up out front of the store, Bob walked out. "Hadn't eat have you?"

"Naw."

"Come on, Kathy has steak, biscuits and gravy. An Bill let it slip so I'm thinking she also has plum pudding."

As they walked into the café, everyone in the place clapped and said howdy to David. He and Bob said howdy and took a table as one of the men said, "Well fellers, it looks like we have ourselves a town hero."

Men agreed as another said, "Yeah, outlaws had better ride around our town from now on."

Bill walked over and took their order with David asking what was going on. Bill smiled, "You mean y'all hadn't read today's newspaper?"

"No."

"Well here it is. Read this while I get yore dinner."

Right on the front page, in big letters was how David Graham saved Blake Sawyer's life. Without David's quick thinking and sharp shooting, Blake would have been killed. Four known outlaws rode into town to kill this newspaper man. Without a doubt, our local boy David Graham is a hero.

David looked up at his dad. "Good Lord Dad, what have they gone an done? This not only puts you and me in danger, but the whole town."

Bob stood and called Bill. "Bill, we'll eat later!"

"Why, what's wrong?"

"That newspaper, that's what!"

Bob and David headed for the newspaper office. Barging right in, Blake looked up with a smile, until he saw the faces of his friends. "Bob, David, what's wrong?"

David reached over and picked up a newspaper. "This is what's wrong, Mister Sawyer."

"Wrong! I thought it a right nice piece."

"You just went an told every outlaw in the territory there was a feller here in Chloride that out gunned four of their kind. How long do you think I have before some of um come riding into town to look me up?"

"I, I never thought if that. It's too late to stop it now a bundle was on the morning stage."

David stood there shaking his head. "Lord how I wish Sheriff Dobbs was here. Maybe he will be before real trouble starts. Mister Sawyer, you went an put this whole town in danger. They come for me and bullets will fly, people hurt."

Mister Sawyer saw the fix he had put everyone in. "Maybe I can put out a special edition just for the town's people and tell um to keep quiet about who you are. If nobody pointed you out to strangers and said you was no longer around, they'd just ride on."

"All it will take is one loud mouth, one drunken miner that don't read the paper. Yeah and what about Dad's store sign, Graham & Son Grocery & Mercantile? I'll have to watch every stranger I see not knowing which one came to kill me."

"Why don't you just take that gun off and not wear it any more? Surely they wouldn't shoot an unarmed man."

"Margret was unarmed and outlaws shot her. Without my gun I would be as defenseless as I was the day Margret was shot. With my gun I'll at least have a chance."

"I am truly sorry David. I was so happy to be alive, I

wanted people to know. What can we do, what can I do?"

"I have no idea, but the whole town needs to know to be on the look out for strangers wearing guns."

"But what if you went away for awhile? You know, just until things die down."

"No, we don't know how long it will be before someone shows up or even if they will. I'll just go on with my normal life and hope someone warns me about strangers."

A week later, Dick and Albert rode into Durango, Colorado. They and the horses were tired after the long trip. After leaving the horses in the livery, they got a room and took hot baths.

Two hours later they were eating supper in a small café. Several men and women sat around with supper before them. As Albert cut into his steak, he glanced up and saw the sheriff and a deputy as they walked through the door.

Howdies were said back and forth, as they took the table right next to Dick and Albert. Both boys very slowly removed the thongs from the hammers of their pistols.

After their meal was served, the sheriff and deputy ate and talked. Dick got the sheriff's attention and said, "Howdy, me and my friend here are strangers to this country. You wouldn't happen to know of a ranch around here what's looking for a couple of punchers."

"Naw haven't heard of nobody needing hands, but if I's you I head on up the valley north, toward Silverton. They's several big ranches up that'a way."

"Thanks, we'll do that come morning."

At this very moment, Jeff and Edgar were outside the cave, eating beans and hardtack. "You're feeling a whole lot better, so I guess I'd better head into town for more supplies. We'll be running low fore to awful long. I just hope Dick an Albert kept on riding and hadn't been caught."

"Yeah it was getting time for us to split up anyway. All law will be looking for four fellers riding together."

"Yeah cept in Chloride, they'll be looking for anybody they don't know."

"Yeah but Jeff, they might have posters out on us. They might know you right off. You could get yore self caught then what would I do? Why don't you just go on off up the mountain to the west er south and maybe get us a deer, er hell even a rabbit er two would help."

"Yeah I guess we can hold out till yer ready to ride."

The evening stage pulled into the B Bar S Ranch and the horses were taken care of before everyone went in to supper. The driver had handed Jim the mail as he had stepped from the driver's seat. Jim took it on inside.

As everyone finished supper, Sherilie had placed the mail beside Buffalo's plate. He picked up the Chloride Miner's Newspaper and thumbed through it. "Hey Shorty, look at this front page."

He handed the paper to Shorty as the stage driver said, "Yeah, that boy is the talk of the town. Saved the editor's life with a new gun is what's said. Four outlaws came into town gunning for him and would'a had him if not for that boy."

Shorty read the complete story with a frown on his face. Buffalo looked up, "What's wrong, Shorty."

"This is a hell of a way to repay somebody that just went an saved yore life!"

"What'd ya mean, how's that?"

"That stupid idiot just went and let every gun slinger in the country know a young boy took out four outlaws at one time and saved that editor. There'll be hell to pay over what he wrote. That kid's life ain't worth a plug nickel.

"Tomorrow I ride. I just hope I'm not too late."

CHAPTER SIX

Morning light found Shorty on his way to Chloride. Dunnie seemed to feel the urgency and loped right along. Shorty talked to himself, almost out aloud. *'That paper is only about a week old, just maybe I'll make it in time. I just hope that boy knows the danger that editor put him in.'*

Leaving Durango, Dick and Albert were headed north up the winding canyon leading over the mountain toward Silverton. After a few miles they could tell that sheriff had been right. This was a beautiful canyon valley and they could see the first ranch house and barns. Cattle and horses were grazing everywhere in fenced pastures.

Dick kept his horse headed up the stage road, riding past the lane leading down to the ranch. Albert looked over at him. "That looks like a right nice place, why don't we try there?" He sounded almost disappointed.

"We ain't stopping nowhere within a hundred miles of the New Mexico border. We'll ride on through Silverton and over the mountains toward Montrose and maybe on north of there. We've gotta find a ranch that's a long way from any town. Maybe stay out'a towns for even a year."

"You think it'll be that long fore they stop looking."

"Might, we just ain't gonna take no chances. Dad gum it Albert, I know we ain't killed nobody, but the law won't look at it that'a way. We was with Jeff an Edgar when they did and we was all seen. It can't be changed now, but oh Lord how I wosh we'd never started robbing. We all had good jobs an didn't need to do it. I ought'a knowed sooner er later somebody would be shot. It could'a been any of us. I lay awake some nights thinking of that teller. Did he have a family? What if he had kids to raise.

"Yeah, and what about that right pretty girl? You know her folks will never get over losing her. That poor girl. Lord if only we hadn't run after Jeff robbed that feller. We wadn't there an had nothing to do with that."

Albert looked over at him, as the horses slowly walked along. "Yeah a friend robbing a man for forty-five cents got us on this outlaw trail. Don't fret none Dick, fretting don't do no good. We'll make out an never go on the owl hoot trail again." He reached his hand over for a shake. "Let's make a oath to each other right now. No more robbing er doing wrong, not ever again."

They shook hands and both felt somewhat better. Two days later they rode into the small town of Montrose. This was right in the middle of Colorado farming and ranching country. Surely some ranch in this country needed good, hard working cowboys.

Around three that afternoon, Shorty rode up the street in Chloride. Going straight to the sheriff's office, Sheriff Dobbs stood and stuck out his hand. "Shorty Thompson! Good to see you. You back down for some more outlaws?"

"Might be, just thought I'd better come down and hang around awhile. I figger that kid David Graham is in for a hell of a lot of trouble. What kind of kid is he? Not some hot head that's quick on the trigger?"

"Naw, anything but that. He's a hard working little feller. He's never give the law no trouble. But I think yer right as trouble will sure be looking him up."

"Why in the world would that newspaper feller write up something like that?"

"Wadn't thinking. He's a right nice feller, an was just glad David saved his life. He thought he was just letting people know what kind of a boy he is. It sure wadn't meant to put his life in danger."

"Let's just hope not too many outlaws read the

Chloride Miner's News. It's been over a week so if any are gonna start showing up, it should be within the next day er two, maybe a week at the most."

"Yeah most outlaws won't even read about it, it will just be told in every bar and saloon in the territory."

"Yeah, that's what I'm afraid of. It'll be built up making this kid a fast gunslinger. There'll be men here to prove he ain't fast an they're better'n him."

"Well, you want to go over to the store an meet him?"

"Yeah, but I need to take care of Dunnie first."

After Dunnie was in a stall eating, Shorty and Sheriff Dobbs walked down to talk with David. The sheriff introduced Bob and Shorty then asked where David is. "He's out back helping unload a freight wagon. Just go out that back door."

As Shorty and the sheriff walked out, a freighter handed David a barrel of pickles and said howdy to the sheriff. David placed the pickles on the loading dock and stuck his hand out to Shorty as he was introduced.

"What er you doing off down this'a way, Marshal? I saw you that time you got them two outlaws right out yonder in the street."

"Yeah, that was a spell back. I'm here checking to see how much trouble has come your way."

"None yet, but I shor have a bad feeling its coming."

"Yeah I know what you mean. I'm gonna be around town for awhile, so if anything does start to happen er strangers show up, back off and get help."

"Yes Sir, I'll do that."

Shorty and the sheriff started to walk off when Shorty looked at David's right hip. "Say David, what kind of a gun is that? It looks new to me, never seen one quite like it."

"Yeah, it's new alright. Here, but be almighty careful, just pulling up on the trigger guard will fire a round."

He handed his rifle to Shorty and watched as he looked

it over. "Now I sure like the looks of this, where can I get one?" Shorty handed it back and watched as David slipped it into the clips of the holster."

"Wait a minute! Where'd you come up with a holster like that?"

"Um, ah made it just for this rifle."

"Are you any good with it?"

"Yes Sir."

"Is there a place around here close where we can go and pop off a few shots?"

"Yes Sir, there is an old mine slag pile where I always go. We close the store at six, if you drop by we'll go out and you can try it out."

"Thanks, I'd like that."

Before sundown or supper, Shorty got his horse and rode over to the grocery store. He walked with David to the livery to get his horse. Leo already had it saddled, as well as his own. "Figgered I'd ride along."

A short time later, David showed Shorty what he could do with his rifle. With six targets set up, in back of the livery David got all six in a little over one second. Shorty whistled right loud. "Damn! Now that is good shooting. How'd you get so good?"

"Practice and more practice. I'd say I've shot up five boxes of shells just getting so I could hit my target."

"Well by dog you did that alright, and was damn fast about it. Are you sure I can't get me one of those rifles?"

"Yeah the feller what made this one for me is long gone. I think he went back east someplace."

"Well by dog you hang on to that one, I've seen nothing that would even come close. That is a new kind of gun."

Leo glanced over at David then Shorty and said, "Marshal, do you really think something like that would sell?"

"Sell! Hell yes and every lawman west of the Mississippi would buy one, including me."

"If by chance I could find the feller what made that one, what would you pay for one?

"Fifty dollars at least, maybe even more."

"That much? That's double what a rifle goes for."

"Yeah, it'd be well worth it."

A half an hour before sundown, Shorty, David, Leo and Sheriff Dobbs rode out to the slag pile. Setting up several targets, everyone wanted David to show what he could do. The most amazed was Shorty and Sheriff Dobbs. Dobbs looked over at David and his rifle saying, "Hell's fire Boy, I couldn't pull the trigger on my .44 as fast as what you done. Yeah, and you hit a target every time. I might'a got two out'a that bunch at this distance."

Shorty was even more impressed. He had seen fast, straight shooting before, but this ranked right at the top. "David, you need to get yore self a patent on that thing. You'd be a rich man in no time at all."

David glanced over at Leo while talking to Shorty. "Yeah I might one of these days, but I think it needs a lot more testing. Me an Leo will work on it."

They all shot off a few rounds with Shorty besting everyone. Leo said, "Now that's how I'd like to be able to shoot. I guess it takes a steady hand."

Shorty smiled, "Yeah and a damn good eye."

As they rode back to town Leo was riding close to Shorty. "Marshal, do you really think there'd be a use for a rifle like that and anybody but outlaws would buy it?"

"Hell, I ain't no outlaw and I'd be among the first. I'd say there is nothing like it out there an won't be unless David gets his self a patent."

"Marshal, I done it."

"Shorty looked over at him. "Done what?"

"Built that gun."

"You did!"

"Yeah, built it and the holster just for David. I just

Paul L. Thompson

didn't want the word getting out where people would be
bothering me to make them one."

"Leo, a new gun like that ever goes on sale, and the
manufacture couldn't keep up with the orders. You'd need
your patent first then go back east to some big gun outfit.
Hell Winchester, Henry, Sharp, there's so many I can't name
um all. Any of um would take it."

Just as they pulled up in front of the livery Leo asked,
"Did you ever hear of Patterson Firearms Company?"

"Sure have, they make some of the best hand guns and
rifles that a person can buy today. Damned expensive, but
well worth the price."

"That's me."

They dismounted, walking the horses into stalls.
"That's you, what?"

"I am Leo Patterson. My grandpa and father own the
Patterson Firearms Company."

"Then what in the hell are you doing in a small town
in New Mexico?"

"I was in my second year of college in Patterson, New
Jersey and…" Shorty interrupted him,

"You mean the town was named for your family!"

"Yeah my great-great grandpa, but this girl I knew
came up pregnant and she said I was the father. Course I
wasn't, I'd never been with the girl. Dad's lawyer said her
whole family was nothing but gold diggers. Her father got a
lawyer and was going to make me marry her.

"Grandpa and his lawyer thought it best if I high tailed
it to the territories unless I wanted a wife and baby. Grandpa
gave me five thousand dollars and sent me west. I wound up
here and bought the livery from Mister Sands."

"How long ago was that?"

"Two years."

"Two years! Why didn't you go back home? You know
she's give birth way before now."

"Yeah Grandpa wrote me saying it was a boy and also after I left, it finally came out that it was her cousin's baby and they got married well before the baby was born."

"You didn't say why you didn't go back home."

"I like it here, by dogged I really like being a hostler, and smithy. I like taking care of horses and doctoring um and make sure their feet are taken right good care of.

"Another thing, just look at all the friends I have. I really mean good friends that my family's money didn't buy. I've got no better friend than David. We hunt and fish together and sit and talk. I wouldn't have that in New Jersey."

Shorty patted him on the shoulder. "Yer alright Leo, but you think over about getting a patent on that gun. It would not only make you rich, but yore whole family would benefit from making a new gun like that one and they're already set up for making um."

With the horses taken care of, the sheriff had to go by his office before going home to supper. Shorty, Leo and David walked down to Bill and Kathy's for a very good meal. Bob was already there and he introduced Shorty to Bill and Kathy. Again, everyone said Kathy out did herself on that meal. Shorty said he just might hang around a lot longer so he could eat Kathy's cooking.

After the meal, Leo went back to the livery and David and Bob went home. Shorty walked down to the saloon for a couple of beers. The day shift at the mines was just over, so the saloon was full of miners. Shorty stood at the bar, looking around and drinking his beer.

Far back against the northwest wall, two men had a bottle in front of them with heads close together. Shorty turned around facing the bar and asked for another beer. As the bartender put it in front of him Shorty asked, "You wouldn't happen to know when them two fellers at that back table got here?"

The bartender eyed Shorty pretty good then leaned over the counter to take a look at the forty-five on his hip. "Why would you want' a know that?"

"Cause I'm a U S Marshal that came to town to make sure David Graham stays alive."

The bartender stuck his hand across the bar. "Glad yer here Marshal, I'm Douglas Feldman. Them fellers walked in a good twenty minutes ago, just before all these miners did. Think they look like trouble?"

"Could be, they look tired and well healed."

"I thought so to, I already went an sent my slop boy after Sheriff Dobbs."

Shorty had just finished that beer when in walked Sheriff Dobbs. He walked over beside Shorty, as Douglas set two beers in front of them. Dobbs nodded saying, "Doug, what did you find?"

He and Shorty pointed the two men out. Dobbs almost spit his beer on a miner that was walking past. "Damn Shorty, don't you know who them fellers are?"

"Naw, don't recall ever seeing um."

"That Stan Guzman an Odie Felt. They're both gun hands from down around Tucson. I can't think of nothing up this' a way they'd be wanting cept David."

Shorty took a sip of beer then said, "Let's walk over and introduce ourselves." Shorty and Dobbs both removed the thong from the hammers of their pistols.

Slowly walking through the crowd they were standing in front of the table before the men looked up and saw them. Both quickly put their hands on the butt of their guns, before seeing the badge on Dobb's vest.

"Oh howdy Sheriff, you want something?"

"Yes, U S Marshal Shorty Thompson and myself needed to let you know a couple of things."

"Yeah, what's that?"

"If anything at all happens to David Graham or anyone

else in my town, Shorty will be on your trail and so will I even if I have to quit my job to do it."

"Naw now Sheriff, you've got us all wrong. We just wanted to take a look at that gunslinger you have living right here in yore town. We heard he was mighty tough, but we wadn't gotta shoot em er anything like that."

Shorty was looking the men over. "Like the Sheriff said, anything happens to that boy an you've got me to contend with and you damn shor wouldn't want that. You run back for Arizona and I'll wire U S Marshal Hopper Scranton just incase you were able to get that far."

"No trouble from us Sheriff, Marshal. You have our word on that."

"I'll believe that when I see you ride out of town."

They walked back to the bar and finished their beers. Shorty was going across the street for a room, but before Dobbs went back home, he would drop by and let David and Bob know trouble was in town.

Stan and Odie had their heads together. "What'da think Odie? Think that sheriff an marshal will be after us?"

"Yeah most likely, but what can one runt and an old man do against our guns? Yep, fore we leave town we're gonna find out just how tough this town's local hero really is."

"From what that miner told us, he ain't nothing but a sixteen er seventeen year old kid."

"Yeah, but look how fast Bonny was at that age. Some kids are just born to a gun."

"Think we ought'a call it off?"

"Naw, no matter how fast he is, he can't get us both."

"Yeah yer right, I'm gonna get us a room an we'll get some shut eye. Come morning we may be high tailing it out'a here. Oh, what about the horses?"

"We'd better take um to the livery fore its too late."
They took the bottle with them going for their horses.

Paul L. Thompson

Walking down the street, they walked right past Graham & Son's Grocery & Mercantile.

"Looks like we know where to find him."

Leo had just closed the livery door, as they walked up with the horses. "Got a couple stalls?"

"Yeah, just for tonight?"

"Just tonight."

They stalled the horses then walked back to the saloon and got a room. They lit a lamp and took the cork from the whisky bottle. After Stan took a long swallow, he handed it to Odie and said, "We need to have our horses ready to ride fore we finish the job. You have um across the street an I'll gun him down an we'll ride the hell out'a here fore the sheriff an marshal knows anything about it."

"Why can't I be the one that gets him?"

"We've gone over this before an we both think I could be a tad faster than you are."

"Yeah yer right, but I'll be ready just incase he gets you." Odie thought a minute. "What if he gets us both?"

Stan laughed right out loud. "You don't think that any more than I do. It'd take a damn good gun to take either one of us, and none could get us both."

They were up a half hour after sunup and walked down stairs to eat. There wasn't over a half dozen men with hangovers eating breakfast in the saloon. The cook cooked and waited on tables. He would set plates of food in front of men then grab the coffee pot filling cups. No bartender was around at this hour.

Forty-five minutes later, Stan and Odie went to the livery and saddled their horses. Walking and leading the horses, they tied up across the street from the grocery. Odie looked around saying, "What if the sheriff er marshal sees us waiting out here?"

"They won't, but if they do we'll handle them too. We came too damn far not to get this feller."

Less than fifteen minutes later, David and Bob walked from the store, headed for Bill and Kathy's. As they stepped from the walkway, David saw two men across the street. One started walking his way. "Dad, out of the way, here comes that trouble!" David moved his right hand to touch the butt of his rifle. Bob quickly went back inside for his own gun.

Stan stopped in the middle of the street and called out, "So yer that fast gun! Think yer faster than a real gun-slinger?"

David was standing exactly the way he wanted to. "You go for that gun and you'll darn shor find out."

As Stan's hand grabbed for his gun, he was slammed back with a bullet in his chest. Odie grabbed for his but saw David was ready to let him have it. He threw his hands in the air screaming, "Don't shoot! Damn it don't shoot!"

Sheriff Dobbs had run from his office at the sound of the shot. Shorty had jumped up from his cup of coffee and out the door of the café. David was walking closer to Odie.

"Mister, with two fingers remove that pistol an let it drop. And so you'll know, if it starts up my way an yer dead!"

Odie was very slow, letting David know the gun would drop. Up ran Sheriff Dobbs with his gun in his hand.

Picking up Odie's gun he said, "Mister, you and Stan was damn stupid! You should'a rode on like I told you to, now Stan's dead an yer going to jail."

"Jail! Fer what, I ain't done nothing!"

"I'm trying to save yore life, you blooming idiot! Look around and tell me what you see."

Odie slowly let his eyes go up and down the street and back. Men were in back of him and all around, with cocked guns in their hands. Odie swallowed hard as he looked Dobbs in the eyes. "Damn, what's all this?"

"A town that will kill you and any of your kind that

comes in here thinking you can kill David and get away with it. Now move!"

"Yeah, yeah jail looks mighty good to me."

Everyone including Bob slowly let the hammers down on rifles and pistols. Shorty walked up to David. "You all right?"

"Yeah an Shorty, I told him not to touch his gun."

"You did the right thing and after me an Dobbs get through talking with Odie, I don't think you'll have much more trouble."

David and Bob went on to Kathy's for breakfast while Shorty walked over to the jail. Dobbs had just slammed the door shut on Odie and was getting ready to hang the key back on the peg.

"Melton lets talk with him and show him the errors of his ways." They walked back to the cell. Shorty caught hold of the bars and stood looking at Odie for most of a full minute. "Odie, what in the hell was you an Stan thinking when you rode in here thinking you could just kill that boy and get away with it?"

"We figgered if we could get him first, it'd make things a little safer for ever body."

"Why in the hell would you think that? He wasn't going anywhere except right here in this town."

"Yeah but he could'a, we just wadn't gonna take no chance. There'll be more boys riding in once I don't get back an tell ever body he's not dead."

"Oh but you're gonna do just that."

"What? You mean yer gonna let me go?"

"Yep just as soon as I tell you a few things and you let it soak into that thick skull of yours."

"You can't tell me nothing I don't already know."

"Oh but I think I can. As your hand touched the butt of your gun, did you see how many town people had theirs on you? Anything happen to David, just one shot fired and that man or men will never ride out of this town. These people will kill you and not think twice."

"So what er you saying?"

"I'm saying yer gonna ride and any low life you see, you tell them about this town. If they don't stay clear and go ahead and feel brave enough to ride in, they won't be riding out. This town looks out for strangers."

"All right I'll do it, but don't know how much good it'll do. There's a bunch of fellers what don't like to hear of a fast new gun. Worries um somewhat."

"They'd better be worried about this one. Alright Melton, let him out."

Melton opened the door saying, "Odie I'm telling you straight. I'm spreading the word, you show yore self back here they are to shoot you on sight an anybody riding with you. Now get!"

"What about Stan's horse an gear?"

"That stays with the town, pays for the burying."

CHAPTER SEVEN

Edgar was feeling stronger every day and Jeff was taking him for long walks down the trail and close to the cave. Getting back around noon, Edgar said he was hungry. Jeff picked up his rifle. "You go ahead and get a fire built. I'll go out here a couple hundred yards and get us a rabbit."

Around thirty minutes later, a rifle shot was heard. Edgar smiled and grabbed the skillet. But Edgar wasn't the only one that heard that shot. Odie was riding over the mountains going where he thought would keep law off his trail, as he made his way to Kingston. He was planning on cutting back south within the next hour.

At the sound of the shot, he waited and listened. It didn't sound more than a couple hundred yards away. *'Now who in the hell can that be? I know the boys are waiting in Kingston.'*

He dismounted and walked on, leading the horse. A hundred or so yards later, he smelled wood smoke and meat cooking. *'Must be a mine up here close.'*

He removed the thong from the hammer of his revolver and led the horse with his left hand. A very short distance later he heard muffled voices. Pulling his gun, he cocked it and brought it up to firing level.

Just as he saw two young men at a dinner fire, one of their horses raised its head and gave out a long whiney. Edgar lay down but Jeff grabbed his rifle looking all around. "Edgar, crawl back in the cave on hands and knees, don't get to your feet you'd make too big'a target."

Jeff scooted behind a large boulder, watching to see which way the horses were looking. Southeast, Jeff slowly eyed every foot of ground and out through the trees.

Odie could tell these were young fellows and wouldn't be after him. He called out, "Hello the camp! I'm one man, can I ride in?"

Jeff looked toward the voice, but talked over his shoulder to Edgar. "Hold your rifle on anybody you see. I gotta let him come in so we can take a look at him. He hollered, "Yeah come on in, no gun in yore hand!"

Jeff kept his rifle where he could drop down and get off a shot in an instant. Odie came walking up, leading his horse. "Heard a shot a bit ago an figgered somebody was about. How about a cup of that coffee I smell?"

"Shor, tie yer horse over there at the corral."

Jeff kept his rifle in his right hand, finger close to the trigger. Odie turned from tying his horses saying, "No need in that gun boy, I'm running from the law too."

"What makes you think we'd be running from the law?"

"You shor's hell ain't miners! Cowboys wouldn't be up in this country hiding out less they's running."

He poured himself a cup of coffee and dropped down on a rock the boys had rolled over for a stool. "Rabbit smells good, got any to spare?"

"When it gets done, yeah."

"Then sit down boy, don't let it burn. And you boy, you in the mine. You can take that gun off me an come on out. I wadn't bull shitting you one pound about me being run off by the law. I'd guess you know that little town of Chloride, well a kid shot and killed my partner an the law locked me up. When they let me out they told me to ride and never come back an show my face er I'd be dead."

"Why did a kid kill yore partner?"

"Cause we heard he was a fast gun an rode in to take him out. Fast! Damn right he was! He had on a new kind of gun. It didn't even look like he had to pull the trigger on."

"Bull shit! There ain't no such gun like that!"

"Yeah there is, just one an I saw it in action. Fore this week is out, I'm gonna have me that gun."

"How'er you gonna do that if the law said you's dead if you showed your face again?"

"Got me five riding buddies what's waiting on me an Stan to get back to Kingston. When I ride in an let um know what happened to Stan, and what he was shot with, they'll help me get it. Yeah, be more'n glad to."

The rabbit was done so they all ate and drink coffee. "From looking at all that horse shit there in that lot, I'd say you boys been here awhile."

"Yeah, well over a month. Edgar there took a bullet last time we's in Chloride. Just now healing up enough to ride, if we ride easy like that is."

"Damn, I wonder if it was that same kid what shot Stan."

Jeff and Edgar both knew to say nothing about robbing the bank, as both their saddlebags were still full of money. "Could'a been we didn't get a good look at ever who it was. Edgar was shot in the back."

"Shot in the back! Now that's a low life polecat that'd do a thing like that. You gonna go back an make it right?"

"Naw, like I said, we didn't see who done it. When we ride out'a here we're headed for Arizona."

"Now Boy, less you ride the Mogollon, south of there is almighty dry an water is hard to find. You go, stay north."

"Yeah we was planning on Prescott er north of there."

"It's too late for me to make Kingston today, would it be alright if I just stayed here till morning?"

"Yeah, but we don't have much coffee er grub left."

"I've got me an Stan's grub, its a few cans of beans, hardtack an a good dab of coffee. I can leave that with you, as I can make Kingston fore I have to eat again. I'll be there by late evening."

"That'd shor be a help and'll let us stay here a few

more days then what we was thinking. Want'a walk out there a ways with me and get us a couple more rabbits for supper?"

"Yeah may's well an when we get back, I've got nigh on to a full bottle of whiskey in my saddlebags."

Morning came and they ate beans, hardtack and drank coffee. Odie saddled his horse, getting ready to ride. He reached into his saddlebags and brought out six cans of beans, a can of peaches and almost a full sack of coffee. "That ought'a last you boys till Edgar is ready to ride. I'll be back in Chloride with the boys in a couple er three days. Anybody in town you'd want me to say howdy too?" He had a broad grin on his face.

Jeff looked up and saw the smile, "Naw, but we shor do thank you fer the grub. Might get to pay you back one of these days."

"Might, after I get that gun from that kid, we'll damn shor have to ride. Might just be Prescott. Well, luck to you."

He turned his horse south as Jeff called out, "Yeah and you keep an eye open."

He and Edgar stood watching him ride until he was out of sight. "Edgar, I shor hope the hell yer fit to ride."

"Why's that?"

"Cause we're getting everything ready and pulling out at daylight in the morning."

"Why er we gonna do that? We've got grub now?"

"Cause when Odie and his friends get through with Chloride they'll ride right in here and the law will be on their tails. We just ain't gonna be here."

"I'm fit enough, but which way are we heading?"

"North, we'll make Magdalena then ride east to Socorro and up the Rio Grande."

All that day Jeff and Edgar got everything ready, putting food and supplies in gunny sacks that could be tied on top of their bedrolls behind the saddle.

Odie pushed his horse to the limit and rode into Kingston after sundown, but before it was completely dark. Dismounting in front of the saloon, he rubbed his back and ass, as it felt as if he was still in the saddle.

Walking through the door, he looked around until he saw the boys at a back table playing poker. As he walked up he was asked, "Where's Stan?"

'Dead, shot dead."

"You mean that fast gun really was fast!"

"Yeah, damn fast. Hand me a swig offen that bottle an I'll tell y'all about it an what we're gonna do."

Odie was poured a glass of whiskey and when half of that was gone he told about Stan, the kid and the gun. "Now I'm telling you, that gun looked to be fourteen er so inches long, no more and he just popped it into his hands. Stan was dead just as he cleared leather.

"Now we're gonna ride in there and get that gun, it's mine. It can be done if we do it right."

"Now wait just a damn minute, we have other things to do sides riding fifty miles for a damn gun."

"John, you ain't seen nothing like this one ever. It's a new kind of gun that would give us the edge on any law that came looking."

They sat around drinking and playing cards until most to mid-night. John looked at the clock above the bar saying, "I'm hitting the sack. Odie, we'll talk more on that gun after breakfast in the morning."

"Yeah, that's what I's thinking, when we all have clear heads and after a good night's sleep."

* * * *

Dick and Albert were at a table in the bunkhouse of the Goss Ranch which was thirty miles northwest of Rifle, Colorado. There three more cowboys also held cards in their hands. "Two bits to you Dick. You in er out?"

Dick smiled as he leaned back. I'm out, as I can see duce's don't have a chance at that pot. I'm hitting that cot an get some shut eye. I've got a twenty-five mile ride tomorrow. The ramrod is sending me an Albert to the north line camp."

Rayland spoke up as he dragged in the pot. "Yeah, you boys got a whole bunch of branding, cutting and de-horning to do. Them boys over there will be glad for the help. Y'all will be eating mountain oysters fer a week."

"Yeah, I just hope the cook knows what he's doing."

"Oh she does, she's a good'un. That's why I wish I's going with y'all. Y'all won't be back for a good month."

"She's! You mean they have a woman cook!"

"Yeah and a pretty little filly she is. But don't go getting any ideas after you see her. She's the daughter of the line camp boss an he's mean'ern a constipated Mountain Lion."

"Yeah, glad we was told about that. What's her name?"

"Nell, Nell McGregor." John looked over at Dick before adding. "Now y'all will cross the road leading from Rifle to Meeker maybe eight er so miles north of Rifle. Don't let the call of town an women let you think you can ride in there fore going on to camp. Y'all have a day off coming in a couple weeks er so. Curly will let y'all ride in after yer paid."

As the sun came over the mountains, Dick and Albert were at least six or seven miles east, northeast of headquarters, loping along. "Well Albert, we've been here a little over two weeks, how do you like it?"

"I do, yeah really do. The boss and all the hands seem easy going. I like doing a good day's work."

"Yeah, me too. I think we'll stay right here as long as they'll have us."

"Mighty fine by me, I like this life."

"You mean even better than what we was doing?" He smiled, looking over at his brother."

"Yeah, an we ain't got Jeff an Edgar, er even law to worry about all the way out here."

"Yeah an no matter what, we're keeping our pact. No more damn breaking the law, not ever."

"Yes we are an no we ain't. When do you think it'll be safe to ride into town an send Mama some money?"

"A while yet, yeah a good while."

* * * *

Jeff and Edgar had rode away from their hideout right after sunup, headed most too due north. It felt good to be in the saddle again. Edgar looked over at Jeff and asked, "Where do you think we'll wind up?"

"No idea, but we can't stay in this territory. There's bound to be papers out on us by now. With all the money we already had and now that bank money, we won't have to be worrying none an having to rob a stage er nothing like that."

"What'da ya think happened to Dick an Albert?"

"No idea, but I hope they made it. We's gonna have to split up with um sooner er later anyhow. Dick was getting pretty touchy about me killing that teller an you shooting that girl. Hell, you know I've always said kill um all that way they can't say who we was."

"Yeah I'm with you on that, but you know that was pretty good of um to pull the law offen us while I was shot. I couldn't have out run no posse. We'd been caught for sure."

"Yeah, I know."

Just before half way to noon, Dick and Albert topped a low hill and saw the road they were to cross. Looking south toward Rifle, there looked to be a covered wagon stopped off to the west side of the road. They were what they figured to be six to eight hundred yards away, but could clearly see only one horse eating grass twenty or so yards away from the wagon.

"Let's ride down an see if them folks need help. Maybe one of their horses died er something."

They angled to the right and loped up close. A dead camp fire still had a coffee pot and skillet setting on rocks. "Hello the wagon!"

With no answer, they rode closer. "What'da you think Dick?" At that very moment they heard a groan and a muffled woman's scream. "Come on Dick, she sounds in trouble!"

They dismounted, drawing their guns. "Albert, keep yer eyes open." Dick, with a cocked gun in his hand slowly opened the flap on the back of the wagon.

At first he saw no one, but heard a moan and looked at a small bed. A woman could be seen. He stepped on in and saw her good. She was lying there eyes closed, face and hair wet with sweat. "Ma'am can you hear me."

Her eyes popped open showing fear. "Yer, yer not a doctor! Where is my husband?"

"I don't know Ma'am. Me an my brother was just riding past and heard…"

She let out with another moan then screamed, placing her forearm over her mouth so it was muffled. Dick saw the raised blanket and knew she was about to give birth.

"Ma'am, I've done a lot of birthing calves an fouls, but never a baby, but you look like you need help."

"Yer not a doctor! What can you do? Oh, ooohhh Lord help me! Please help me! Help me now!"

"You take it easy an I'll do what I can." He turned back and looked through the wagon flap. "Albert, get a fire built and water on to heat. This woman is about to have a baby."

Albert looked all around, "Will both our canteens be enough?"

"That looks like a water barrel on the side of the wagon, see if there's any water in it."

He turned back to the woman. "Ma'am, yer gonna have that baby an I'm gonna help. Now you put this rag in yore mouth so yore screaming won't bust my ears."

He pulled back the blanket and saw the bed was wet and there was the top of a small head trying to be pushed through the opening.

"Now Ma'am, with yore hands grab hold of them bed post and push with all yore might. If you can just get the head free, I'll give you a hand."

She pushed, twisted and pushed while screaming into the rag. With the third push the head came out all the way to the baby's neck. "Alright, I'm gonna pull just slightly and you push again. We've got to get the shoulders out next."

He put his right hand under the side of the baby's head and said, "Alright, push, push. Keep pushing its coming! Push harder, a little more, just a little more. There, I've got my hands under the arms. One more push and we've got it."

As she pushed, the baby slid into Dick's hands. "Darn Ma'am, hold on just a minute!" He got his knife and wiped it on the bed cover then cut and tied the cord. Lifting the baby, he handed it to her saying, "We're heating water that ought'a be warm enough right now."

He called from the wagon, "Albert! I need that water, now!" He reached as Albert handed him a pan over half full of water. Getting what looked like a clean rag, he washed the baby and did a good job. "Ma'am I'll get clean water if you think you can clean yore self up."

"Yes, please."

He had Albert empty the pan and refill it. Setting it where the woman could reach it he said, "I'll just wait right outside. Now you call out if you need me."

He stepped out of the wagon and asked Albert if he had coffee ready.

"Yeah, here's a cup. What was it, a boy er girl?"

"A boy and sure is a big um. Him and his mama is gonna be just alright. She said her husband rode to Rifle for the doctor and left before sunup. Now I'm thinking he ought'a been back way fore now. I'll stay here an you ride in an see if you can find him. Ask the doctor, maybe he's see him."

Elbert got his horse and rode off in a hurry. Just as he got out of sight, the woman called out, "You can come in now."

Dick stepped back in the wagon and took the pan of water and emptied it. Going back in he asked, "How are you feeling?"

"Fine, much better thanks to you. I know I could never have done it without your help. What is your name?"

"Dick an my brother Albert went looking for your husband. I'll just wait here till he gets back. Would you like a cup of coffee?"

"My goodness yes! I am also hungry if you could fix us a bite to eat."

"I'll get yore coffee first."

They drank coffee and talked while the baby nursed. "Are you and your brother from around here?"

"Yes Ma'am, we work for the Goss Ranch. Were you and your husband headed for Rifle?"

"Yes we were. He came all the way up to Meeker two days ago to get me. We will be living in Rifle. My husband was just two weeks ago given the job of sheriff in Rifle. We thought the baby would hold off another week or so, but you see what happened."

They heard horses coming up, so Dick went to see if it was Albert and her husband. It was and the man was off the horses running to the wagon. Dick stepped out of the way as the man lunged inside.

Dick went on out to talk with his brother. "Where'd you find him?"

"He was coming on this'a way. He said he'd rode on south of Rifle looking for the doctor, but couldn't find him so he was coming back to see if there was anything he could do for his wife. You about ready to ride?"

"Yeah, reckon so." As he reached for his horse's reins, the man stepped from the wagon.

"I sure want to thank you for all you did. My wife told me everything. By the way, I'm Ronald Young, called Ron an I'm the new sheriff of Rifle. Anytime yer down there, stop by my office and say hello."

"Well Sheriff, we'll just do that. It's best we ride, it's gonna be dark now fore we get to north camp."

They started to ride off when Ron called after them, "Oh I almost forgot! My wife named the baby Dick. Thought you'd like to know."

Dick turned in the saddle smiling, "Thanks."

CHAPTER EIGHT

O die, John and four other men rode to within a mile and a half of Chloride, by-passing the Thomas farm. Odie turned his horse west saying, "I know of a little creek southwest of town a good mile er so. When we ride we'll be riding out that'a way anyhow. There's a couple of cowboys that are staying at an old mine up yonder on that mountain. They won't mind the company."

They rode another couple of miles before coming to the creek. "We'll camp right here. Now John, when you an Hugo go in there after a bit, it'll be coming on dark. Look ever thing over and that kid and his old man own the grocery and mercantile. I think they live in back, so you'll have to watch an see when the kid comes out by his self. I think he's too young to go in a saloon."

They set up camp and built a fire for coffee. Everyone except John and Hugo unsaddled their horses. About a half an hour later John said, "Alright Hugo, let's ride." They started for their horses.

Odie said, "Hold it! You can't go in there wearing guns they'll be on you fore you even dismount."

"What in the hell are you talking about? I ain't riding nowhere without my gun!"

"Damn it John, the whole town is looking out for strangers. You ride in there healed, you'll never get close to that kid. Just roll your gun and holster and put um in yore saddlebags."

Less than an hour later, they walked into the saloon. At the bar they called for a bottle. As John paid, he saw most every man in the place was giving them the eye ball pretty good. They walked to a table and pulled out chairs. As they dropped down, Hugo asked a fellow at the next table, "What in the hell is ever body looking at? Ain't they ever seen tired cowboys before?"

The miner didn't smile as he said, "Nothing meant by it. We're just careful of all strangers. We see y'all don't wear guns so you'll be left alone."

"Good, we didn't ride in looking for trouble. What in the hell is ever body so nervous about?"

"This town don't want no gunslingers coming in here causing trouble. They do, they'll not ride out."

"Yeah I see ever body is wearing guns cept you an a couple more. Why ain't you wearing one?"

"We're miners, so we leave um at home."

John and Hugo had a couple of drinks before asking the bartender if he had any rooms. "Naw full up, but down the street is the hotel, I'm sure they have some."

"Where's the grocery store? We're gonna need a dab of grub fore we ride out."

"It's across the street from the hotel. Now I reckon you'll be wanting breakfast come morning. Right next door to the hotel is Kathy and Bill's café. You'll not find better grub nowhere."

"Thanks." Hugo looked over at John and let a slight smile come to his lips. "While we look things over tomorrow, we'll go in and get plenty of grub for the boys. One of us will take it out to um and let Odie know what we found out."

"Yeah, I just hope Odie wadn't feeding us a line of horse shit about that gun. But by damned I shor want'a see it."

They left taking the bottle with them. Walking, leading the horses they walked right past the grocery then turned across the street for the hotel. After getting a room, they asked where the livery was.

"It's up the street two and a half blocks, but Leo has closed for the night. You'll have to take your horses around back of the livery and put them in the lot. If they fight other horses that wouldn't be a good idea. Might get um shot."

"Naw they don't fight." They took care of the horses, throwing the saddles over the fence and taking their saddle-bags with them to the room.

Before sunup, they were up and John looked out the window and across the street at the grocery store. "Hugo, you stay here and watch that grocery while I go to the outhouse. When I get back you can go."

John was back in fifteen minutes and Hugo started to turn from the window when Bob and David walked out the front door. "Take a look John."

He walked over and saw a man and boy coming across the street. "Hell they're going to the café for breakfast, come on!"

Bob and David already had a table and Bill was pouring them coffee, as John and Hugo walked in.

Bill looked up and saw two men he'd not seen before, but they weren't wearing guns. "Take any table, need coffee?"

"Yeah, thanks." They sit and Bill filled their cups. "What'll you have?"

"Biscuits, gravy and scrambled eggs."

"Want any ham er bacon with that?"

"Yeah, ham."

Bob and David had only glanced over at them as the café started filling up with customers. Both John and Hugo tried getting a look at David's right leg, but was too far to the left.

Bill was serving their breakfast, when in walked Sheriff Dobbs, and U S Marshal Shorty Thompson. They made their way to Bob and David's table.

"Look at that, Hugo."

"Yeah, looks like that kid has his self a U S Marshal looking after him."

"We don't know that, he could just be here."

John and Hugo were through eating well before David and Bob finished. They had several more cups of coffee, waiting. At last Bob got up and told Shorty and Dobbs he would see them later then paid for their meal. David stood and turned to say howdy to a couple of men. John almost dropped his cup and bumped Hugo's knee with his own. They watched as David and Bob left.

John paid their bill and walked out, standing on the walkway watching David disappear into the store. "Damn Hugo, Odie was right! I've never seen a gun like that and that kid wears it like he knows how to use it. We'll have to be careful of him an the law."

"Yeah, how'er we gonna go about getting it without getting shot? If not by him then that sheriff er marshal."

"I'm planning on that right now. Might take longer than I was thinking. Let's go over an get the horses and pay for their keep, then go get that grub. I want'a talk with that boy."

Leo said he noticed the saddles and extra horses. "Want me to throw um a dab of hay?"

"Naw, we have to use um right off but'll be back later."

"Then how about four bits?"

John paid and they saddled the horses and rode to the grocery. Going inside, only Bob was behind the counter. He looked up, "What'll it be fellers?"

"Sack of them hardtacks, a dozen cans of beans, two pounds of jerky and five pounds of ground coffee. Oh and a slab of bacon if you've got any."

"Yes Sir, I can fix you right up." He called over his shoulder, "David, bring me a slab of that lean bacon!"

As Bob stacked things on the counter, David walked from the back room with the bacon. John saw the gun and how it was strapped to David's leg. "My goodness Boy, what in the world is that thing you have strapped to your leg?"

"It's my rifle."

"Rifle! Come on, that don't look like no rifle to me."

"Well it is." David walked back into the store room.

John and Hugo paid for the supplies and put them behind their saddles. Riding east from town, they circled back to the camp and waiting men. Odie was the first to hear them coming.

He was like a kid waiting for candy. As they rode up he asked, "Did you get it? Where's it at?"

John stepped from the saddle saying, "Hell no we ain't got it yet, but we will. I saw it strapped to that kid's leg an yer right, there ain't another like it. Now that is some new gun alright."

"How'er you figgering on getting it?"

"We was in the store, oh, you boys unload that grub. We got plenty for when we pull out. Now what I'm gonna do is get right friendly with that boy and when nobody else is around I'll knock a fire ball out of him and get his rifle."

Odie was almost rubbing his hands together. "Now it'd be best if you didn't kill him. Law will quit looking a lot sooner if you don't. An that's a good hideout them two cowboys are using."

"It'd better be, after seeing that rifle an all that law I figger we'll have to hole up damn near as long as if we robbed that bank. That kid an ever how many he can get will come looking. Yeah and most likely that U S Marshal."

They stayed around camp until late in the evening then went back into town. Tying the horses close to the saloon, but not right in front, they went in for a drink. As they bellied up to the bar, there stood Shorty and Sheriff Dobbs with their backs to them.

They didn't get a bottle this time and only had one drink. Getting the horses they walked up to the grocery and walked in saying they had forgotten tobacco. As Bob handed him the two bags of Bull Durham, John paid the dime and asked, "Where's that boy of yours? I thought maybe he'd have time to show me that rifle of his. You wouldn't happen to have one around here for sale?"

"Naw, that rifle was made special. David went out to the Thomas place to see Margret. Ought'a be back fore dark."

"The Thomas place, ain't that out east?"

"Naw, south a couple of miles."

"Thanks, we'll see yore boy tomorrow fore we pull out."

It was just sundown, but nowhere near dark as they loped the horses, headed south. Not much more than a quarter mile later, they saw a horse loping their way.

"That's gotta be him. You ride upon one side and I'll be on the other. No matter which one of us he talks to, the other one will cold cock him. Just make damn shor he don't get a chance of getting to that gun." They slowed the horses to a walk.

David pulled to a stop right between them. "Howdy fellers, y'all riding out this late?"

Hugo answered, "Yeah we've got miles to put behind us fore it gets too awfuldark."

"This road don't go nowhere cept the Thomas place."

"Yeah but we're gonna cut west…"

John blind sided David with a powerful right fist. David never knew what hit him as he was knocked off his horse and onto the hard road. Both men were off their horses and on David like a mountain lion on a new born fawn.

While they removed the rifle from David's waist and right leg, Hugo reached into their saddlebags for their pistols. John stood and strapped the rifle to his own leg. Popping it in and out of the holster, he couldn't believe what a good job was done."

"Come on, let's get the hell out's here!"

They rode west toward their camp. David's horse had stood over to one side then started nibbling grass as the two men rode off. It was a good fifteen minutes before David started moving and getting to his knees. Seeing his horse, he slowly stood and picked up the reins. Mounting was hard, as he was still dizzy. Though it was not much more than a quarter mile to town, it took him twenty or so minutes.

As he rode up in front of the store, Bob had just closed and turned and asked, "How's Margret and Seth doing?"

He looked up and saw David was still dazed. "What happened, Son?"

"Them two men that came in and got grub an that lean bacon, they slugged me an took my rifle."

"They did! Come on, we'll tell Melton and maybe find Shorty. Wait, I'll do that while you go ahead and take yore horse over to Leo before he closes."

As Bob went for Dobbs and Shorty, John and Hugo rode into camp. Odie walked over beside the horses as they dismounted. With a smile he said it looked like they got the gun. "You didn't have to kill the boy, did you?"

"Naw, just put him to sleep." John stepped around looking Odie right in the eyes.

Odie saw that and asked, "What?"

"I'm keeping the gun."

"Yer gonna shit too! By damned that's my…"

John shot him right in the heart. He laughed, "I couldn't let a little piss ant like him get hold of a gun like this. He'd thought he was a big man."

Hugo asked, "Yeah but where do we go now? He was the only one that knowed about that mine where we could hide out for awhile. We've gotta be out'a here come daylight."

"Hell he said it was upon the side of that mountain. We'll just watch for tracks an foller um."

It was dark when Jeff and Edgar rode up to the livery in Socorro. "Stall, feed an water um. Where's the hotel?"

"Down the street a couple of blocks."

"Thanks, we'll pick um up after breakfast in the morning."

They took their saddlebags with them to the hotel. After getting a room, they asked where the closest café was. "Two doors down, they close in another hour."

As they headed for the café, the night clerk quickly reached under his desk and brought out several posters. The third and forth ones he looked at, he knew these were two of the wanted boys.

Stepping to the door, he looked down toward the café but saw no one. He hot footed it across the plaza to the sheriff's office.

"Ramon, these two just walked in and got their selves a room. They're in the café right now." He handed over the posters.

The sheriff was on his feet pushing the clerk toward the door. "Hurry, I'll be waiting in their room when they walk in. Just don't you act all nervous and give everything away."

"I won't, I want that five hundred dollar reward."

"If this is them, you'll get it."

Thirty minutes later, Jeff and Edgar walked back in the hotel. As they started for the stairs the clerk asked, "Y'all want a wake up call in the morning?"

"Naw, we'll be up."

Getting to the room door, Jeff opened it and Edgar followed him inside. Striking a match to light the lamp, they heard a hammer being brought back to full cock. Both hit the floor grabbing for their guns at the same time. Fire leaped four inched from the sheriff's gun as Jeff pulled the trigger at the flash and kept pulling the trigger until his gun was empty.

He heard no sound and said, "Don't shoot, I'm lighting the lamp." As light flooded the room, there lay Edgar with a bullet in his throat. The sheriff was also dead.

Grabbing both sets of saddlebags, though it was empty, he still held his pistol in his right hand and slowly backed out the door and turned just as the clerk pulled both triggers on a double barreled shotgun. Jeff was blown off his feet, almost cut in half.

The clerk walked on in the room and saw the sheriff was dead as well as the other boy. Going back to his desk, he laid the empty shotgun on the counter and walked out the door.

Walking to the saloon, he asked the bartender where the deputy was. "Roberto just went to the outhouse. What is wrong, you look pale."

"Ramon is dead."

"Dead! What happened?"

As the clerk started to tell what had gone on, in walked the deputy. The clerk told him Ramon was dead, as they walked back to the hotel. The deputy kneeled down beside the sheriff's body. "He is not dead, go for the doctor, now!"

As the clerk ran from the room, the deputy poured a bowl of water from the pitcher and started washing Ramon's face. It was a good ten minutes or better before the doctor rushed in."

Feeling for a pulse, he told the clerk to go get two more lamps while he and Roberto lifted Ramon upon the bed. "Roberto, you get the lamps and tell Horace to start heating water, a lot of water. While it is heating, tell him to go over and get Rosa. She must know."

"Will he live, will he live?"

"I will do what I can, but everyone must pray."

As the doctor worked to save Ramon, the clerk and Roberto cleaned up the mess in the hallway and had the undertaker and his help carry out the bodies of Jeff and Edgar.

The clerk held up both sets of saddlebags. "Roberto, these are full of money."

"It must belong to the bank in Chloride. After we see if Ramon makes it, I'll take it over there and get your reward."

It was every bit of two hours by the time the doctor had taken two slugs from Ramon's body and sewed up the holes. "Rosa, I want you to stay by his side. If you have to go to the toilet, holler for Horace to stay with him until you return. I will get some sleep but come back in the morning."

Rosa had a pleading look as she asked, "Tell me doctor, should I get the Priest? Will my Ramon live?"

"I have done all I can. It is now up to him and God. If they both have the will, he will live."

The next morning after breakfast, the doctor walked to the hotel to check on Ramon. John, Hugo and the other three men were making their way to the mine where Odie told the cowboys were hiding out.

Shorty, Melton, Leo and David rode to where the two men had jumped David and taken his rifle. Leo and Shorty both said they were leaving an easy trail. Less than a half hour later, Shorty was feeling warm coals of a dead camp fire.

There lay Odie, dead. "This one Melton had in jail after I killed his partner. The two that slugged me had been in the store a couple of times. Sure got a gob of trail grub like they'd be by-passing towns for awhile."

"This one was shot before he could even start for his gun. It looks like the two fellers with your gun met up with this one an three more then stayed the night right here. Maybe that's why they got so much grub. Now they're headed for Diamond Peak. They must be going over the mountain and head to Silver City. As plain as this trail is, they must think nobody will be after um for awhile. Maybe they think they killed David. Let's ride, but everybody eye ball the terrain in front of us. They may just be suckering anybody that gets on a trail into a bushwhack."

David looked over at Shorty as they all mounted. "Yeah, why didn't they just shoot me?"

"I'd say they didn't want nobody to hear the shot."

The trail led in and out of canyons climbing higher and higher. By mid-morning John saw horse corrals before seeing the mine. "Well this looks like it, but I don't think the cowboys are around. Don, you an Artie get wood for a fire and get coffee water on. We'll put the horses in the lot."

Hugo was looking all around. "Wonder where the cowboys got off to. This looks like a good hideout."

"Yeah, but we ain't staying all that long. We'll pull out come morning." They unsaddled horses and drank coffee before John said he was going to try out that new rifle.

It took several minutes before he figured out how to get it free of the holding clips with any speed. After a bit he was like a kid with a new toy. He just couldn't stop firing and reloading.

Hugo reached over saying he'd like to try it. "Yeah, but you remember, it's mine. There won't be nobody that can go against us now. I guess I really do have to thank Odie for that."

Before half the men had tried the rifle, their shots were heard by Shorty and the men with him. "Alright, it looks like they've stopped for awhile. We'll leave the horses here where theirs won't hear us. Everybody take extra cartridges and keep quiet. As many as there is we'd be in for it. We'll look the situation over before splitting up."

Ten minutes later they were within a hundred and fifty yards of the five men. They were sitting around a fire with a coffee pot at the edge of the fire. In a whisper Shorty said, "Only that big feller has a gun across his lap and the other rifles are on them saddles leaned against the fence.

"David, can you tell if that's your gun er not?"

"Yeah and that feller has my holster on his right leg."

"Okay Melton, how do you want to go about this?"

"Well these two boys here are both damn good with their rifles. Let's put them where they can already have a bead on the one with David's gun and the one next to him. You and me can pick out a couple more after we get in a bit closer. There looks to be plenty of cover to within seventy-five to a hundred yards.

"I'll holler out they're under arrest then all hell will break loose. Now David, you an Leo shoot to kill. The quicker they're dead, the less chance of one of us getting shot. How's that sound, Shorty? You figgering anything else?"

"Naw, but so you know which one I'll take out first, it's the one closest to the mine."

They snuck as close as they though they could without being heard and spread out about ten feet apart. Just as Melton started to call out, two of the horses lifted their heads and looked their way. The fellow closest to the mine stood and followed their gaze.

John asked, "What'da ya hear?"

"Nothing, but the horses know there's something out there." Everyone looked at the horses then southeast. "Naw guess it's nothing, might'a been a wolf er some varmint."

Just as they sit back down, Melton yelled out. "Yer covered, don't move!"

Every man jumped up grabbing for his gun. Forgetting the new rifle was empty, John swung it around just as a bullet took him right between the eyes. Shots were fired at unseen targets, but only the Sheriff's men hit what they were aiming at. In less than fifteen seconds it was all over. Five men lay dead.

CHAPTER NINE

Just over three weeks of working cattle, Curly said the men could ride into Rifle, but had to be back to work day after tomorrow. "We've gotta get these cattle back out yonder on grass. Now Nell and Sam are taking the wagon for supplies. If they need help I expect you boys to lend a hand. Line up and get paid."

As each man got his thirty-five dollars, Curly thanked them for a job well done. Dick and Albert were the last in line, because they were the newest hands. "Dick, you and your brother here showed some of the other hands how it's done. I want to thank you for that. Y'all ride, rope and cut right with the best. With y'all here we damn near cut a week off this round up. Don't go to getting drunk and forget to come back, there's still work to do."

"Thanks Curly, yer a good man to work for. We'll be back."

With the supply wagon along, it took until late getting to town. Everyone, including Nell got rooms first thing. Sam drove the wagon over in front of the grocery store. He and Nell went in and gave the man their order. "We'll be picking this up after breakfast in the morning."

"Thanks Sam, Nell. The order will be ready anytime you are. If you like I can have every thing stacked by the back door. I built me a loading ramp back there. Makes fer easier loading wagons."

"Thanks, I'll take the wagon around back in the morning."

Sam and Nell walked out front and stood on the walkway. "Sam, you go ahead, I've got to get me a few things at the dress shop an dry goods."

"Dress shop! You don't wear dresses!"

"No but I darn shor wear bloomers!"

"Uh, oh yeah. You go ahead and I'll just take the wagon an horses to the livery then check on the boys in the saloon."

About half of the ten cowboys that came to town already had them a woman and were up stairs, by the time Sam walked in and saw Dick and Albert sitting with four more hands at a large table. One of them looked up and called out, "Come on over Sam, help us drain this bottle fore it gets stale."

Sam got a glass from the bar and took the chair beside Dick. "I figgered you boys would be knuckle deep in a poker game."

"Yeah maybe later, right now we're just resting and enjoying the noise. Shor is different than hearing a bunch of cows bawl."

He looked around, "The other boys up stairs?"

"Yeah. ought'a be down after a bit. You gonna have you a woman while yer here?"

"Yeah may's well. It's been a spell since I's in a town."

Dick said he and Albert were going to find a café and eat a bite before drinking too much. Sam said that was a good idea, he'd just go with them. "You boys coming?"

"Naw, we'll grab a bite of something after we get us a woman. We can eat anytime, a woman we need worse right now."

As Dick, Albert and Sam walked out the door, four rough, dirty looking men walked in. Everyone had a low gun hanging on their hips. As they walked toward the café Sam said, "Now that's trouble if I ever saw any."

Just before getting to the café, Nell called out for them to wait up. "Darn Sam, y'all was gonna go eat without me."

"Yeah, I didn't know how long it'd take you to buy bloomers an we was getting mighty hungry."

Nell blushed and quickly looked at Dick. He just opened the café door and stepped back for the others to walk in first. They took a table close to the window where Dick held Nell's chair for her. From here they could look out on the street. Dick smiled, telling Nell she sure looked nice, as he took the chair next to her.

"Well I bought myself a new outfit and took a bath. Now I'm starving." When Sam was looking for the waiter, Nell smiled right sweet at dick.

"Dick, thank you for noticing I'd changed clothes."

Their meal had just been set before them when through the door walked Sheriff Young and his wife carrying a baby and also a very pretty girl was along that looked to be about seventeen. At seeing Dick and Albert, they walked right over. Dick, Albert and Sam stood. Ron already had his hand out to Dick.

"It sure is good to see you fellers. As you can see Dick and Mary are both doing just fine." Everyone was introduced and the pretty girl was Ron's sister-in-law.

Ron helped his wife into a chair at the next table, where they could talk for awhile. The girl's name was Rachel and she sat where she could see Albert, very clearly. Albert thought she sure had a beautiful smile and pretty long hair.

Nell was the most impressed when she found out why the baby was named Dick. "You never told us nothing about that!"

"No need, wadn't nothing to it. We just done what anybody would have. We just happened to be there but Mary did most of the work, I just caught it."

Mary added, "I think he saved mine and my baby's life. I know I couldn't have done it without him. I had already given up."

They all finished their meals and talked. As Dick and everyone at his table got up to leave, Ron stood with his hand out again. "Again thank you for what you did. Anytime yer in town, please drop by the office and we'll go out to the house so you can see the baby."

"Thank you, I'll be shor an do that."

Albert said how nice it was seeing the baby and Mary again, and meeting Rachel. Rachel asked, "When Dick comes to see the baby, do you think you will be along?"

"I shor hope so, but it might be another month. Bye now."

As they walked out, Rachel caught her sister's hand. "I really think Albert is cute, don't you?"

"I suppose so. He sure caught your eye."

"I really think both those brothers are very polite and nice."

Ron laughed, "Yes, they are very nice gentlemen."

Sam was leading the way back toward the saloon, when Nell asked Dick, "Do you have to go back in there with them?"

"I reckon so I don't have anything else to do."

"I thought maybe you'd go with me for a walk down along the creek. I mean if you'd want to."

"Do I! I mean shor I'd like that. Albert y'all go ahead and I'll see you later."

Nell said, "Much later, like at the hotel. He'll be too busy for any more drinking tonight."

Sam heard every word, but just smiled to himself as he and Albert walked on. It was just a short walk to the creek, and was a beautiful setting. Nell wasn't looking at Dick as she said, "I just love this place. I go for a walk every time I come to town."

"Alone?"

"What do you mean, alone?"

"Do you come down here and walk alone?"

"I most certainly do, who do you think I would walk with?"

"I don't know, maybe some feller."

"I don't got no feller! When do you think I have time for a feller? Good Lord I work all the time and am glued out at that line camp. Once er twice a month we come in for supplies."

"What about maybe one of the boys?"

"Well I'll be dogged! Yer jealous and hadn't even knowed me a month!" She reached, pulling his head down into a long sweet kiss. When she stepped back she smiled, "I like you too Dick Boggs."

The kiss almost took his breath. "What'll Curly say when he finds out I kissed you?"

"Well if he finds out, and I'm certainly not going to tell him, I'd never get to kiss you again."

"Why not?"

"You'd be dead."

"Dead!" He stepped back about a foot.

She laughed out loud. "I'm just fooling you. He wouldn't kill you but he might run you off."

"Then we'll have to be mighty careful. Now that I've got you, I don't want to turn loose."

"You won't have to. I know how to act around him and the other men. We'll act as we always have, they'll not know nothing, that is if can keep my hands off you." She kissed him again then took his hand, as they walked on down the creek. A couple of hours later, the moon came over the mountains and it was a very beautiful night.

They made it back to the hotel before any of the men. Dick walked her to her room and started to walk down the hall to his, but she held him one more time. "It's going to be real easy getting use to you. You are what I've been waiting for."

"I never even thought much about girls, till you." He kissed her again and squeezed her hand. "See you at breakfast."

The next morning just at sunup, Sam and Nell were on the wagon seat as they slowly left town with the load of supplies. All the other cowboys, except Dick and Albert would stay in town another day and night before riding back to the line camp.

Sam almost snickered to himself at what he was about to say, but said it anyway. "Dick, I thought you an Albert would'a stayed in town with the boys an finished twisting off. You know, maybe even had yore selves a woman. Be another month fore you get back to town." He almost laughed out loud.

"Naw we don't drink all that much cause it's hard sitting a hoss with a headache after drinking a gob. I've never been with a woman. And I need to get on back an oil my gear anyway."

Sam glanced over at him. "Yeah, I noticed you only had one beer an didn't have time to have yore self a woman. Oiling that gear must be important. Now fer a cowboy what don't get to town all that often, that's kind'a strange. I mean don't you think so? I mean you do like women, don't you?"

"Yeah, oh yeah I really like women, it's just that… Well it's… Darn it Sam you know what I'm talking."

"Yeah I guess you've got yoreself a gal back home, ever where that's at."

"No darn it! That ain't what I mean at all…" He brought his horse to a stop, thinking then caught up. "Sam, me an Albert need to ride back to the post office. We was gonna send Mama some money an near plumb forgot. We'll catch up in a mile er two."

They rode back and tied up in front of the post office. "Albert, you send Mama what money you think you can spare an I'm gonna send that little bank in Alma what we took from them. That banker said that was all the money that town had."

Albert went on in the post office, but Dick walked to

the grocery and got a small box. Going back to his saddle-bags, he looked all around as he reached in and got a couple thousand dollars. Putting it in the box, there was still room, it wasn't full. He looked around and found two paper bags. On one of the bags he wrote, Sorry. Folding them just right, he placed that on top.

He walked inside and addressed the box to: Bank, Alma, New Mexico Territory. Then he showed it to the post master. "Will the bank get this?"

"Sure, if there is only one bank in Alma."

"Yeah, only one."

"Want to put a return address on this?"

"Naw, I don't have one. We're just riding."

"Well don't worry, Boy. It'll get there in about a week er so."

"A week! Is that all?"

"Yeah, it'll be put on a train the first town where there is one. Then go by stagecoach the rest of the way."

They got their horses and kicked them into a long lope. Dick looked over at Albert. "How much did you send Mama?"

"A little over two thousand, that ought'a last a good while. But I still got plenty left. An Dick, I'm glad you sent that bank some money, even though we didn't get even a thousand from it."

"Yeah me too, I think they needed it worse than we do."

Nell heard them riding up so she turned and smiled. As they rode beside the wagon Sam said, "That didn't take long."

"Naw, just figgered it time to send our mama a dab of money. We don't need much working on ranches."

Sam smiled, "Yeah an you shor don't spend much when you do go to town. Not even on a woman, that's hard to believe." He glanced at Nell who was giving him the evil eye.

Nell stood and hollered over at Albert, "You want'a ride in the wagon and let me ride yore horse?"

"Shor." He rode up close and just stepped into the wagon bed, handing Nell the reins. She jumped into the saddle and slowed the horse to ride beside Dick.

After a couple hundred yards and not looking at one another, Nell asked, "Did you really mean it when you said you'd never been with a woman?"

"Yeah, why is that so hard to believe?"

"Well I've heard the hands talking when they come back from town. They're always talking about the women they humped. Yeah even before they go, that's all they talk about is getting a woman before getting too drunk er doing anything else."

He looked over at her thinking of what to say. "Nell, my mama always told me an Albert not to go around humping women unless we was gonna marry um. She said not knowing you could leave some girl an later she'd have yore baby and you'd know nothing about it. If she was doing favors for money, how could she raise a baby?"

"Well other cowboys do it and think nothing about it."

"Is that what you expect me to do? Every time I go to town, get me a woman? Will that make me more one of the boys?"

"No, no that's not what I meant at all. I just wondered if you did it, that's all."

"I will when I marry and not before. Now let's not talk no more about it."

She smiled and said, "Yer strange Dick Boggs, yes you are."

"Good er bad strange?"

"Good."

It was middle afternoon by the time they made it back to the line camp. Curly and the men that hadn't gone to town were in the corral doctoring a couple of calves.

Curly told the men to finish, as he walked on over to the shack to help with unloading the supplies. He was surprised to see Dick and Albert saying, "How come y'all are back? Run out'a money?"

"Naw, just figgered we'd get on back and get our gear oiled up while we had the chance."

"Well help with these groceries before taking care of your horses. Sam'll need help with the team."

With everything in the shack, Sam, Dick and Albert took the horses to the barn to unsaddle and unharness them. Curly stayed with Nell and as they put things away, said he liked her new outfit.

"Papa, of all the men only David even noticed I had new clothes on and said I looked nice."

"Well by dogged you do look nice. What did you do with yore self last night while the boys an Sam was in the saloon?"

"Me an David went walking along the creek."

"You did! Why would he do that stead of drinking an playing poker? I know they ain't been to town to twist off none."

"I asked him to walk with me and he said yeah, he'd druther do that than go back in the saloon an drink."

"He did! I'll have to have a talk with that boy."

Nell quickly thought she had told her father too much about Dick and he would suspect she and him had something going."

"Why do you need to talk with him?"

"Maybe he's sick, you know, coming down with something. Every cowboy I know can't wait to get to town for women, whiskey and poker. Yeah I'll bet that's it, he's feeling poorly. Him and that brother of his are darn good hands. I don't want either of them coming down with something."

Nell breathed easier and Curly headed for the barn. She quickly started getting ready to cook supper. She stopped, thinking a moment. *'Yes, Dick is different than other cowboys. I pray he is the one I've been waiting for.'*

* * * *

Two poorly dressed Mexicans came leading their burro into Chloride. Stopping at the livery, in broken English they asked Leo if he had any work they could do to get a bit of grain for Roscoe. Leo felt sorry for the skinny animal and said he would feed him.

Both Mexicans bowed and thanked him. Then they asked where they might find work of any kind. They could paint a fence or house and do any kind of adobe or rock work. Leo looked up the street and saw at least a half dozen buildings that needed painting. "Ask the owner of every unpainted building you see. Surely someone will want their place painted. Yeah and when you look down an alley and see junk stacked up, go in and see if the owner wants it took to the dump."

The two walked off smiling to themselves. They walked around town looking everything and everyone over. Stopping in front of the Graham & Son Grocery and Mercantile, they watched people come and go before walking inside. "Jerky."

Bob handed them a large bag saying that would be ten cents. As one man paid he asked, "You got work?"

Bob thought a minute before saying, "Yes by jacks I do! Come on out back and I'll show you what I need done."

Bob showed them how he wanted the yard cleaned and barrels stacked against the fence. They were also to clean and rearrange the storage shed.

When David walked into the store and didn't see his dad, he walked out back to see Bob giving a couple of Mexicans instructions about cleaning. "You didn't have to hire them Pop, I'd got to it after a bit."

Bob walked over to David saying, "Yeah but it looked as if they could use a little money."

Both men had stopped and looked at David's right leg and the gun strapped to it. Bob and David walked on into the store leaving the men to their work. Making sure they couldn't be heard, one said to the other. "That was the gun. What if he wears it all the time?" He rolled a barrel over close to the fence.

"We will find where he sleeps and take it early enough we will have time to ride far away. Two days or three and we will be in El Paso and get our two hundred American dollars."

They worked all that afternoon and one went in and asked Bob if he had anything else for them to do. While he was talking, the other one sneaked into the house and found what he thought was David's room. Going over, he made sure the window would open without a squeak.

He got back to the yard just as Bob walked out with his friend. Bob looked all around and smiled. "Good job fellows, good job. If you come back around noon tomorrow, I have a freight wagon coming in and you can help unload."

"*Si Señor,* we do that."

"All right, here's two dollars for today's work."

"*Gracias, donar agua?*"

"What's that?"

"May we have water?"

"Oh yeah shor, come on inside."

Bob gave them a drink and said he would see them tomorrow. David was stacking canned food on shelves and asked, "They do a good job?"

"You bet, right good. They'll be back tomorrow and help unload that freight wagon, if it comes in."

The two Mexicans walked slowly around town before walking off toward the creek, looking over their shoulders to make sure they weren't followed. At the creek they walked west for most of a quarter mile before coming to their camp. "Edwardo, you water the horses while I build a fire for coffee."

"Mateo, what you think of the gun we see?"

"It is as Mister Carlson said it would be. I have never seen one like it. But for two hundred American dollars, I would even take the boy back to El Paso with us."

"Why do he say we don't kill him and take the gun?"

"He say taking a gun we go to jail. Killing the boy we hang. That is if we get caught."

"But we don't get caught. Let's kill him anyway."

"No his father was a very nice man that give us work, thinking he was helping two poor men. He is good I would not want to break his heart. Maybe he never help no one again."

"Mateo you are getting soft. We will never see these gringos again, what do you care if the old man helps someone else?"

"So Edwardo, that is the way you would repay kindness. No, I will go in and get the gun. That way I will know the boy stays alive, unhurt."

Before dark, but well after sundown they saddled their horses and cleared camp. Waiting until almost mid-night, they slowly rode back to town and about a hundred yards behind the house. No light was seen, so Mateo dismounted and handed Edwardo the reins.

"If I am caught, you ride back to where we was camped and wait until I am out of jail. If I am not caught I will be back in about a quarter hour. No matter, do not fire your gun at anyone. If you are seen, ride away."

Mateo made his way to the window and found it open. Slowly, ever so slowly he eased over the sill and without a sound placed one foot on the floor, then the other. With a moon shining outside, and through the window, it only took a minute for his eyes to get use to the dark room.

Hanging on the bed post at the foot of the bed, the gun and holster was easy to see. As he lifted it free, his eyes never left the sleeping boy. As he back stepped to the window, not one board squeaked to give him away. Once away from the house, he ran the rest of the way to the horses and Edwardo.

"Why you run? Did he almost catched you?"

"No, I was very quiet. If a mouse had been in the room, he would have made the noise of a stampede compared to me. We must ride hard and find a place to hole up and sleep a few hours."

With the horses tied to a stump, Mateo and Edwardo were sound asleep under a tree, ten miles south of Chloride. David awoke and started to dress. With his pants, shirt and boots on he reached to the bedpost. His gun was gone.

He walked into the kitchen where Bob had coffee ready and was cooking breakfast. "Pop, what did you do with my rifle?"

"Your rifle? I never touched it."

"It's gone!" He rushed back to the bedroom and looked all around. Before heading back to the kitchen, he saw the open window. Walking over he stuck his head out and looked all around. As he went through the kitchen and out the back door he called over his shoulder. "I'm gonna see if they left tracks."

In the soft dirt behind the house, he saw foot prints, but they weren't boot tracks. He called Bob out to take a look. Bob got down on one knee and looked the tracks over. "Let's go to the yard behind the store. I think I can match these prints."

Sure enough, right where the two Mexican men worked, foot prints that were exactly alike. "It was them two Mexicans. They wore shoes with a smooth sole. Why in the world would they take yore rifle?"

David started for the kitchen door saying, "Lets get

breakfast over with then I'm going after Shorty and Leo. Maybe between us we can foller these tracks to where they had horses waiting."

"Leo was saying they only brought in a burro when they got into town. They didn't have any horses."

"Well they can't get far on or leading a burro."

Thirty minutes later David was in the sheriff's office asking where Shorty was. "He's at the livery saddling his horse. He's headed home this morning."

David asked the sheriff to come with him. As they walked to the livery, David told him what had happened. Shorty had Dunnie saddled and was talking with Leo. When he heard David's rifle was missing again, he mumbled to himself, *'Damn, I thought this was over.'* "Let's go look at them foot prints you saw."

Leo said the burro was still out back in the lot. They all followed foot prints to where two horses stood and one of them had taken a crap. Leo felt one of the horse turds saying they were at least five or six hours old, maybe a bit more.

"I'd say somewhere around mid-night, there a'bouts."

"David, get yore horse and canteen. Yeah and stick a rifle in that saddle scabbard. May as well take along a dab of trail grub, no telling how far we'll have to go this time."

"Then yer going with me?"

"Yeah, it's a cinch somebody that knowed about that rifle sent them Mexkins after it. They was also smart enough to know gunslingers might'a had trouble."

Leo asked, "Shorty would it be alright if I tagged along?"

"Yeah shor thing, be glad to have you but what about yore livery? No telling how long we'll be gone."

"I'll get Bud Beal to take care of it while I'm gone."

CHAPTER TEN

As they got ready to ride, the morning stage pulled out headed for Winston. Sheriff Dobbs asked if Shorty thought he should go along. "Naw, the three of us ought'a handle a couple of Mexkins." The banker came running up.

"Sheriff! Hold up a minute an look what came in on the stage last night." He handed Dobbs a small bank bag.

"Money? Was that all? Who sent it?"

"The deputy over at Socorro, he sent a note saying two men was killed over there and we had posters out on um. He hung on to it for awhile thinking he was gonna bring it, but the sheriff was shot up by them two and he still wasn't up and around very good yet."

"I'd say them are the two that robbed the bank the last time, but I wonder where them other two got off to."

"He sent no word about any other men, but did say one of them had been wounded before and was still healing up. He must have been the one I shot."

With supplies in saddlebags and canteens filled, Shorty, David and Leo took up the trail of two Mexicans. It was close to eight-o-clock as they rode south by southeast from Chloride.

Mateo and Edwardo were still asleep, ten miles away. Shorty kept the dun to a long lope, following two horses. The trail was easy to follow, but he didn't want to lose it by going too fast.

Leo called over, "Hey Shorty, they don't seem to be in no hurry. We might just catch up fore too long."

"Yeah but they was riding in the dark when they left. I'd say right about now they're making up lost time."

Mateo had just opened his eyes and got up to take a leak. He called over his shoulder, "Edwardo, get up and make some coffee. We slept too long, it is already late. When we are finished with coffee, we will ride to the river and water the horses. If we hurry we can make El Paso in two or three days."

Edwardo talked as he took his leak. "It is much too far to the river. We must ride on south to that little stream. The horses must have water soon."

"You are right and it is not out of the way." They built a fire and drank coffee, but were in the saddles in less than a half hour. They had no idea three men were riding hard on their trail and were now less than a mile back.

They rode in a slow lope and an hour later, were watering the horses from the Seco Creek. Both dismounted and got their own drink before filling their canteens. "Hey Mateo, how long to the river would you think?"

"It will be close to night fall, but we will make Hatch by tomorrow night. We will have us some tequila and maybe a woman. We will have to keep the gun with us so it is not stolen."

They rode just off the south side of the creek, headed southeast. Edwardo looked over at Mateo and asked, "Why you think a gringo would give so much money for a rifle that is all cut up. What good is it?"

"That I do not know. I would not want one."

"Nor would I."

Shorty, David and Leo got to the creek about fifteen minutes after Mateo and Edwardo had rode off. As they watered the horses, Leo was looking at the tracks. "Hey Shorty, these tracks are only minutes old. Looks as if we've gained a good bit."

"Yeah I saw that. We'd better keep an eye out, although I'd not think they're watching their back trail."

David asked why Shorty thought that. "Because they

could have spotted us as we rode over that last hill."

"Maybe they did and are headed for the river."

"Naw, they only have the horses in a slow lope."

"Think we'll catch um in the next little bit?"

"Could."

Within the next hour, Shorty spotted two riders loping along less than a quarter mile ahead. "Well there they are."

David started to kick his horse out saying, "Come on, we'll get um now!"

"Hold on David, sure we could get these two, but ever who sent um would just send more men when these didn't come back with the rifle."

"Then what'er we gonna do?"

"Foller um and get the coward that sent um."

Leo asked if Shorty thought that might be in Mexico. "Could be, but I'm thinking more like Las Cruces er maybe El Paso. They get the Chloride paper in both places, but not in Mexico."

They slowed their horses and followed along behind all day. An hour before sundown, the river was in sight. Shorty reached into his saddlebags and brought out his binoculars. "Well they're just watering the horses and filling canteens. I'd say they're not going to camp this early."

Leo mentioned it might be a dab harder seeing them when they were riding at the same level of elevation. Shorty nodded but said, "Yeah but the stage road has sand in spots and is a lot softer so there's no chance of losing their tracks. I figger they'll ride until dark before stopping."

They watered the horses at the river then rode on south. "We'll have to be careful an not ride upon um. We'll camp back a good ways so they can't see our fire."

"After we camp, are you gonna check um out?"

"Naw not me, I figger Leo could do that and not be heard."

Mateo and Edwardo slept late again and didn't get on

the road until right at sunup. Edwardo asked, "Think we can still make Hatch before dark?"

"Oh yeah, this stage road will make it easy and we won't have to chouse the horses doing it."

"That is good. I am ready for a whole bottle of tequila."

"Si, and a woman."

They picked up their pace to make sure they got to Hatch before dark. Shorty, David and Leo loped along less than a quarter mile back. Around noon, everyone rode to the river to water the horses and fill their canteens with cool water. Leo asked Shorty if he thought they would stay in Hatch tonight.

"Looks like they're trying to make it that far, while it's still light. Now if they do, maybe they'll head for a saloon. I'll go in for a beer and just might get to talk to um. Now both of you will have to stay out of sight, they know y'all."

David asked if they were going to stay at the hotel. "I am you two will camp down by the river. I'll ride out and get you after they move on in the morning."

As they loped along, they met the north bound stage and waved at the driver and shotgun guard. Shorty glanced to the west saying, "You boys had better'd brought yore rain gear. Looks like rain even before we get to Hatch."

An hour later they were riding in a down pour. Leo shouted to be heard above the rain pounding on their slickers. "Think this'll slow um up any?"

"Nope, we only have a mile er so getting to Hatch. I'd say they kicked their horses out a bit and are headed for the livery."

Twenty minutes later they watched through the rain as Mateo and Edwardo left the livery and headed for the saloon. "Come on, we'll see if that hostler will let you boys sleep in his dry hay barn. We need to get the horses fed and rubbed down anyway."

The hostler was a nice fellow and said the hay loft was a darn good bed. After taking care of the horses and getting them in stalls David said, "Hey Shorty, I think me an Leo will head over to that café and get a bite to eat."

"Yeah, let's go. My guts are growling."

As they ate their supper, the rain slacked off then stopped completely. "David, you an Leo stay in that loft until after them two come for their horses in the morning. I'll be right behind them and after we saddle up, we'll go over and eat breakfast before taking up the trail."

Shorty walked up the street to the saloon, walked in and ordered himself a beer. Looking around the bar, there were several tables taken, but only one with two men drinking tequila. As he drank that beer, he watched as one of the men talked with a girl then walked with her to a back room.

Shorty saw David's rifle lying on the table and the other fellow had his left hand on it. He slowly walked over saying howdy. Mateo raised his eyes answering, "*Si,* what you want?"

"Oh nothing, I just noticed yore rifle and wondered what happened to it. Don't look like much of a gun to me. What's it used for?" Shorty watched his face as his eyes dropped to the rifle.

"That I do not know. It is not mine, it belongs to a friend."

"Oh and you're just taking care of it for him."

"*Si,* you can say that."

"I'd sure like to know what he uses it for. Does he live around here close? Maybe he could tell me."

"Naw, he lives in El Paso." Mateo thought Shorty was just a curious cowboy.

"Well by dogged I'll be heading on down to El Paso, does he own a ranch somewhere around there?"

"No, he owns a gun and ammunition store. He repairs and sells all kinds of guns."

"Thanks fellow, maybe I'll look him up when I ride through there." Shorty stuck out his hand. "Shorty Thompson."

"Mateo Silva, have a good night."

"Yeah, you too." Shorty walked back to the bar for another beer. He wondered if he should have pushed it and got the man's name that owned the gun store.

Edwardo walked from a back room, sit down and drank a half glass of tequila. As Mateo got up, Edwardo reached with his left hand and brought the rifle close, leaving his hand on it. Mateo walked to the end of the bar and picked out a woman and headed for a back room. Edwardo poured himself another glass of tequila.

Shorty finished that beer and headed for the livery. Whistling, both David and Leo stuck their heads over the hay loft floor. "What'd you find out, Shorty?"

"I'd have to say neither of these fellers are gunfighters. I just think they are a couple of sneaky thieves and some hombre in El Paso knew that and sent um for the rifle. I didn't get his name, but he owns a gun shop and I'd bet there ain't too many places in El Paso that repairs and sells guns. Well I'm headed for the hotel and grab some shut eye. Y'all remember to wait until they leave before saddling y'alls horses. I'll come in after they leave."

By seven thirty the next morning, they headed for El Paso.

At daybreak that same morning, Dick and Albert rode away from the line camp, on their way back to headquarters. Nell had wanted to grab and kiss Dick, but knew her father would throw a fit. She hollered as they rode away, "I sure hope Mister Goss sends y'all back over here right soon."

Dick turned in the saddle, "Yeah me too."

Curly eased over putting his arm around Nell's shoulder. "Daughter, them are two of the best, hard working cowboys I've ever seen. Next time I have to go over to headquarters, I'm gonna ask the boss if I can have um over here as permanent hands."

"I'd sure like that, pop. They're really nice, not like most cowboys. They don't drink much and carouse when they go to town. You know I've never even heard one of um cuss."

Curly pulled his arm from around her shoulder and asked, "And just what's wrong in a little drinking and carousing?"

She laughed, "Nothing at all Pop, if that's what you want'a do. I just think they are saving their money for something better."

Curly looked after them, "Maybe yer right. They just might make something out'a their selves one day."

They turned back to the barn and walked inside. As Curly saddled his horse, Nell watched, working up her nerve. As he stepped into the saddle she asked, "Pop, what would you say if I told you I really like Dick a lot?"

"I'd say you was plumb dumb if you didn't." He rode off, leaving Nell with her mouth open."

"Well I'll be dogged! Wish I'd knowed he thought that." She walked on inside and started washing breakfast dishes.

About half way back to headquarters, Albert just had to know a thing or two. "Dick, what did you think of our cook? Now I think that little gal shor can put a meal together."

"Yeah, she did alright I guess."

"Alright you guess! Darn it Dick I seen y'all making eyes more'n once. Yeah an sometime when we was all playing poker, I'd look around and you was no where about. When I'd go looking, I couldn't find you er Nell either. What do you say to that?"

"Yer nosy."

"Nosy! Is that all?"

"Yep, that's it."

Paul L. Thompson

They rode into headquarters by middle afternoon and dismounted over by the corral fence where Mister Goss and Alton, the ramrod stood looking at a couple of colts.

As they dismounted Alton asked, "What'er you boys doing back so soon? Get run off?"

"We finished with that roundup, branding and dehorning."

"You did! That's a week er so early, did Curly do a head count? Maybe rustlers are hitting that herd."

"Oh yes Sir, we counted um alright. Curly wadn't sure we got um all but there was sixty four hundred and ninety one mother cows, an just over fourteen hundred bulls."

"How'd the calf crop look?"

"Healthy and strong, but Curly didn't count um all. They was running an playing so much it was too hard to keep count."

"That's right good an that many I'd say no rustlers are about. You boys go ahead and take care of yore horses an let um rest up the rest of the afternoon. I'll get y'all lined out tomorrow."

* * * *

Two hours before sundown, the stage pulled into Alma and the driver handed the postmaster the mail bag. The driver looked around asking, "Any passengers? I've gotta roll if I'm gonna make White Water fore plumb dark."

"Naw, none that I know of."

As the stage pulled out, the postmaster walked back inside, going through the mail. His eyes stopped on a small box addressed to 'Bank, Alma, New Mexico Territory.'

"Now I wonder..." He took the box and headed across the street to the bank. Walking over to the banker's desk he said, "This just came in on the stage."

The banker looked at it and slowly opened it. The

folded brown paper sack with the word sorry was the first thing he saw. Removing it and the other bag, he saw money and glanced up at the postmaster.

As he removed the money and started counting, tears came to his eyes. "Thornton would you look at this! Somebody sent us money, over two thousand dollars."

Thornton asked, "Now who would do such a thing?"

The banker picked up the brown sack and read aloud, 'Sorry'. He looked up at Thornton," You don't suppose them bank robbers had a change of heart, if they did why did they send so much? They only got around eight hundred dollars in that robbery, it was all the money I had. Remember, I had to go over to the bank in White Water and get a loan just to stay open."

Thornton thought a minute before saying, "Yeah it had to be them. I can't think of any body else that would even send money, much less with a note saying sorry."

"You know come to think of it, two of them boys didn't act like they wanted to rob me. Maybe they just needed a loan and was sure they couldn't get one. Now they've paid it back and more. Just a thought, we'll never know for sure."

* * * *

Shorty, David and Leo were only a couple hundred yards behind Mateo and Edwardo, as they rode into El Paso. They started past a livery when Shorty said, "No since taking a chance of them seeing y'all. Go ahead and take care of yore horses. I'll follow these jaspers and see if they're headed for that gun shop."

One block north of the river and Mexico, the two men dismounted at a hitch rail beside a dozen more horses and in front of Carlson's Gun and Ammunition. Not looking around, they disappeared through the door. Shorty rode past then turned his horse back to the livery. David and Leo had their horses unsaddled and were rubbing them down.

As Shorty dismounted he said, "Well I found where they took that rifle. After the two Mexkins leave we'll check it out. We'll have to be careful what we say, there looked to be a dozen er so horses out front. I'd hate to get in a gun fight with that many gun slingers."

At that very moment J R walked from the back room, as Mateo and Edwardo waited at the counter. "Did you get it?"

"Oh *Si Señor*, this is it." He handed the rifle to J R.

"This don't look like much of a gun." He reached for it, gripping it by the lever. As he picked it up putting pressure, the gun fired, hitting one of his men in the right leg. That scared the hell out of everyone.

"What the hell?"

"Why in the hell did you shoot Munce, boss?"

"I didn't... Well I did but I never even put my finger on the trigger." He was very careful as he turned the gun over and over, looking at every inch. "Damn, this thing has a pin that jams up against the firing pin. If I jacked another cartridge into the chamber and pulled up on this it would fire."

"Bull shit! No gun fires with out pulling the trigger."

"Oh yeah, watch this." He slowly jacked in another cartridge. "Now watch this." Very slowly he put his hand through the lever and squeezed it tight. He blew a hole in the floor, scaring everyone again. "What'd I tell you?"

He looked at Mateo and Edwardo. They were as white as the white in their eyes. J R smiled and counted out two hundred dollars. "There you go boys, now get lost."

Neil Kames asked, "Boss, what in the hell are you going to do with a rifle like that?"

"I'm going to make twelve of um. One for each one of you boys. Now with guns like this, there won't be no body that has a chance against us. I'm talking trains, banks and stagecoaches. We'll all have to get use to using a new gun. The fellow that made this one knew what he was doing.

"Come morning we'll ride out to the mountain and do a little target practice. I want to see how it works before copying it. If it works the way I think it will…"

J R Carlson stole guns from the army or anywhere he could get his hands on them. The rifles he made were cheap and almost worthless. Hell they were smooth bore so there was no telling where the lead went after being fired. He sold all he could get his hands on to the Apache and Mexican banditos.

Bert Coswell, thought he was a better gun hand than he really was. He walked over to the counter saying, "Let me see that damn thing." He reached for it, holster and all.

J R spouted off, "Damn it Bert you be careful with that!"

"What the hell, don't you think I know how to use a rifle!"

"Yeah but this one is a new kind of rifle."

"They all shoot!"

He strapped the holster around his waist and tied the thong to his leg. Fumbling and jerking to get it free of the clips, J R hollered, "Damn it Bert…"

Bert put his hand through the lever and jerked. The firing pin slammed into a cartridge, blowing off his right ankle bone. He dropped to the floor screaming his head off. Neil reached down and removed his boot. "Damn! Would you look what he done to his ankle and boot! That damn thing is dangerous. That slug cut that boot like a knife and blowed his ankle bone clean off"

J R unstrapped the contraption from Bert saying, "Just leave it alone damn it! We've all got to get use to it." He looked around, "Jerry, stop that bleeding an somebody go over and get the doc. Both these dummies need patching up."

"It's late, what if he won't come?"

"I said bring him!"

It was a good fifteen minutes before the doctor came in carrying his bag. He dropped to one knee and looked at Bert's ankle. "I can do nothing for that here. A couple of you fellows carry him over to my office."

He walked over to where Munce was sitting in a chair. Looking at the leg he said, "That slug didn't go all the way through. I'd say it hit a bone. Get him over to the office if you want me to work on him. It has to be dug out'a there."

The doc gave Munce chloroform and went to work on his leg. The bullet was embedded in the bone and it was very hard getting it out. He slowly sewed on the hole and bandaged it. Turning to the four men, he told them to go on, it would be tomorrow before they even came to.

It took over two hours working on Bert's ankle. Bone fragments had to be dug out. He bandaged it, knowing after the bleeding stopped and it healed a few days, the whole foot would have to be put in a plaster cast.

It was close to midnight when the doctor got to bed. He knew his morning would start early. As sleep over took him, his mind was wondering how grown men could be so stupid.

The next morning, just as J R opened his store Shorty walked in. He saw several men sitting around drinking coffee and two more behind the counter. "Howdy, I need a box of forty-fives."

J R reached back to a shelf for the cartridges. "That'll be four bits." He noticed Shorty looking at the sawed off rifle and scabbard that was lying on the counter. "Bet you never saw a rifle like that one." He smiled right big at this little cowboy.

"By jacks yer right. What happened to it?"

"Happened to it! Naw, it was made that'a way."

"Bull crap, why would somebody mess up a good rifle. I'd bet it wouldn't shoot a hundred an fifty yards."

"It's not fer far off shooting. It's fer up close, fifty yards er less. If you's right careful I'd let you take a look at it."

He handed the rifle still in the scabbard to Shorty. "Now cowboy, that thing is loaded and has fourteen cartridges in the cylinder. Don't point it at nobody, just the floor er ceiling."

Shorty was very slow taking the rifle. "What kind'a holster is this?" He started it around his waist and every man in the room scattered which brought loud laughter from J R.

"It was special made just for that rifle. Go head and draw it, but point it away from ever body. It has a hair trigger."

Shorty walked toward the left side of the room and only three feet from the door. J R, in his wildest dreams never saw what was coming from this little cowboy. Shorty gripped the stock and acted like he was grunting and pulling to free the rifle from the clips. Looking up at J R he said, "Let me try that again. Now if I do this…"

He popped the rifle free and fired off a round three inches from J R's head. Then in the next split second he fired another round over the heads of the men that were kneeled down out of harms way.

"J R hollered, "That's enough kid! Damn it I said be careful. You like to have blowed my damn head off."

Shorty smiled, "Yep, and the next one is right between yore eyes. "Ever body up! Off that damn floor and put yore hands on that counter." He motioned the gun barrel right at J R. "You too hombre. One wrong move and it'll be yore last."

"Cowboy, you just don't know who in the hell yer messing with! I'll have yore hide nailed to a damn wall!"

"When you come after me, bring all yore boys then count and see how many rides back. You see that nail head over yonder in that wall?"

"Yeah."

Shorty fired. "Now look at it."

Where the nail was, there was now a hole. "That's every time I pull a trigger. I see a head out that door as far as I'm in sight of it, that man is dead."

He slowly eased for the door then said, "Oh, in all the excitement I almost forgot my forty-five cartridges. With the rifle in his right hand, he walked to the counter and got the box of shells.

As he backed toward the door, he noticed a hand easing down toward a gun butt. He shot the gun butt and shattered it. The man's hands shot above his head as he screamed, "Don't shoot, damn it don't shoot."

Every man stood frozen to the very spot, mouths open. Shorty was gone a good three minutes before J R got his wits about him. "Go get that bastard! Damn it he's got my rifle!"

Not one man moved toward the door. "What in the hell's the matter? Go get that rifle back!"

"Now J R, you saw how that little sucker shoots. He could get us all. Yeah an where would we start looking?"

"It's a cinch he ain't from Mexico an we ain't seen him around before. I'd say he'd be riding north come morning and would stay close to water. That means up the Rio Grande, probably on the stage road. I want every stinking one of y'all out there some where and have a trap set up. If he gets away, don't a damn one of y'all come back! You hear me? No body! Now get yore damn horses and ride!"

CHAPTER ELEVEN

D avid and Leo were waiting with saddled horses and were surprised that Shorty came back with the rifle, and this quick. "Damn Shorty, how in the hell did you do that?"

"Right easy, but damn shor dangerous. Get mounted, we've got to get the hell out'a here. That ol' boy has a hell of a lot of gunnies and I'd say could get more if need be. We've gotta stay out'a sight for a spell. One good thing that's on our side they think only one man has got this rifle and I wadn't riding a horse so they won't know what Dunnie looks like. Maybe they won't be looking at three men riding along. Oh, here David. You'd better keep it strapped on cause you'll be needing it before we get clear."

"Are we heading back toward Las Cruces?" They were already in the saddle, headed for the river.

"Yeah but I'd say they ain't stupid and will be on our asses in about five minutes. We could make our best time on the stage road, but I'd say they know that. Let's head for Anthony but watch our backs. We see um coming, we'll change directions."

"Are we going to take the stage road?"

"Nope, that's exactly where they'll set up a trap. We'll ride the west side of the river. It'll take longer but we'll at least make it to Anthony. They'll show up there later this evening."

Neil and Buck Thornton led ten men out into the sand hills north of El Paso, to set up the trap just to the east of the stage road. Both men had seen Shorty use that rifle and knew they had to take him from his saddle without giving him a chance. Buck asked, "Neil, why would you think one little cowboy would go an take a rifle from a room full of armed men? He ought'a knowed we'd come after him."

Neil, sitting behind a large soap weed bush said, "Yeah, he knowed we'd come, but didn't seem to give a shit."

"He had to know he has no chance against twelve guns, didn't he?" Buck was worried, and Neil saw that.

"You know I was thinking, what if he is a gunfighter and not just some lone cowboy wanting a new rifle?"

"Then I'd say our ass's is in trouble. J R could also be in trouble if we don't get him."

"We're gonna get him, don't you go to worrying yore self none about that."

They lay in waiting all morning and until late afternoon. Buck got up and walked out ten or so feet and took a leak. Talking over his shoulder, "You don't suppose he's still in El Paso?"

"Damn it Buck, I don't know where he is, but we'd better find him er J R will have our hides."

As Buck buttoned pants he turned, "You wouldn't think he was on that stagecoach we saw that went by an hour ago?"

Neil stood and looked all around. "Hell yeah! We know he wadn't riding a horse when he came in there an got that rifle. He just waited around and caught the noon stage to Las Cruces." He hollered, "Ever body get mounted. We'll catch him in Las Cruces!"

Two of the men grabbed reins, but before mounting asked, "Neil just asking, but what if he's still in El Paso somewhere?"

Neil stood there a minute then said, "Alright, you an Butler go back and see if you can find him. Now if you do run into him, don't think you can take him. One of you come after us, we'll be riding north. It'd also be best if you didn't let J R see you."

At that very moment, J R and one other man were trying to duplicate what they remembered about the rifle. They had a rifle barrel cut off and the stock was now about five inches long. The man stopped and looked at J R. "What about that pin that released the hammer? How do we do that? Yeah and how are we gonna make that over sized cocking lever?"

J R picked up the sawed off rifle and slung it across the room. "Damn it I don't know, but somebody had it figgered out. Neil had better not show back up here without that rifle." He thought a minute before saying, "Get yore gun strapped on. We're gonna walk this town over just in case he's still here close."

It was coming on to sundown as Shorty, Leo and David rode into Anthony. "Let's get these horses taken care of and get a bite to eat. None of them fellers saw y'all, but I'll have to keep an eye open just incase they show up here."

They were through eating and headed across the street to the bar when ten horsemen slowly rode up the street. Though it was almost dark, Shorty recognized Neil as one of the men in the gun shop. He quickly turned his head and walked toward the walkway in front of the drugstore.

Leo asked where he was going, the bar was farther down. "That's the hombres after that rifle. Y'all watch and see where they tie up. We might have to get on out of town and camp along the river tonight."

Neil and his bunch tied up right in front of the bar Shorty, Leo and David were headed for. David said, "Darn, just a couple of minutes later and we'd been in there. What now?"

Shorty smiled, "Well just maybe I don't need a beer so bad after all. David, why don't you un-strap that rifle and hand it to me. I want y'all to go in there and see what kind of talk you can hear from that bunch. I'd hate leading um right back to Chloride. While y'all do that, I'm going back in the café and drink a dab more coffee and eat a piece of pie."

Leo walked in first with David right on his heals. Standing at the bar Leo asked for a beer. The bartender looked right close at David. "Sarsaparilla for you young fellow?"

"Huh, oh yeah, sarsaparilla is just fine."

The bartender smiled and poured Leo his beer then handed David his sarsaparilla. "That'll be a dime."

They turned and spotted the men at two tables half way across the room. David asked, "How in the heck are we going to hear what they're saying?"

"Come on, we'll take that table right behind um."

Just as they sit down Buck was saying, "Damn it, J R is going to a hell of a lot of trouble trying to get that damn rifle back. That was the sorriest piece of crap I ever laid my eyes on."

"You'd damn shor better not let J R ever hear you say that."

"Well if it's so damn good, why don't the cavalry have a bunch of um? You just tell me that."

"Hell I don't know! Maybe it's one of a kind."

"That's what I'm trying to say. If it was any good, they'd made a gob more of um."

Neil emptied his glass and slowly looked over at Buck. "Come to think of it, you could damn shor be right. Hell J R shot Munce an Bert blowed that own damn ankle plumb off. Now as far as me, if we do get it back I ain't putting my damn hands on it."

"Are we just gonna sit here an get drunk? Where in the hell do we go from here?"

"I'm thinking on that right now. Pour me another drink." He slowly sipped his whiskey with a far away look in his eyes. Suddenly he banged his fist on the table, scaring all the men including Leo and David.

"I've got it! By damned I've got it!"

"Got what?"

"How we can get a gun like that one an take it back to J R."

"What in the double hell are you talking about? We have no idea where or which way that little cowboy went."

"We don't have to find that cowboy. Come morning we're headed for Chloride."

"Chloride! What the hell for?"

"Ever who made that rifle is bound to be still in Chloride. We'll just ride in there and find him. Ten of us, not even the law will mess with us. We'll grab some important looking jasper an make him talk. Ever who made that one will do the same fer us er there'll be a few dead people in Chloride."

Buck quickly said, "Yeah, but once we find out who made it, why stay around a town where anybody could take a pot shot at us. Why don't we just grab him an take him back to J R?"

"Yeah, hell yeah! Now that's thinking, he can make as many as J R wants. Just not one for me though, no Sir not for me."

David and Leo eased away from their table and walked out the door. As they headed for the café Leo said, "Darn it David, it looks like we brought a lot of trouble to Chloride by making that new gun. I shor hope Shorty can think of something."

As they walked into the café to talk with Shorty, J R and Brazil were in an El Paso saloon about half drunk. "Damn it Brazil, I had my hands right on that rifle an let it get plumb away from me. Neil has got to get that cowboy an get it back. I hope they gut shoot that little bastard."

In walked the two men that Neil let go back to El Paso looking for Shorty. At seeing J R, they stopped dead still, but too late. J R had raised his head and saw them. Jumping to his feet he hollered out, "You've got it! Where's it at?"

"Naw Boss we don't got it, we..."

"Damn it I said fer y'all not to show yore faces back here till you brought that rifle!"

"I know Boss, but we was waiting out yonder along the stage road till middle afternoon, then me an Butler came back here looking just incase he never left town. Neil an the rest of the boys rode on north thinking maybe he left here on the stagecoach."

J R glared at them. "Sit down, an you'd damn shor better hope Neil comes back here with that gun!"

David and Leo told Shorty everything they heard in the bar. Shorty leaned back in his chair thinking. "Well fellers, we've gotta stay glued to these hombres. We'll wait until they ride out then foller along behind until they camp for the night. If we can't get um, maybe we can at least cut their horses loose an run um off."

"Yeah but Shorty, sooner er later they're gonna get to Chloride. Why don't we just take um now?"

"Cause there's just too damn many. We could all wind up taking lead. Naw, we'll hang back and keep an eye on um and see if we can't pick off a few lowering the odds."

Neil and the boys stayed drinking for awhile when Neil said, "Buck, here's what I'm thinking. If all of us rode into Chloride, there's bound to be shooting. Being as there's a full moon out there, I want you an Clyde to go on and grab that feller. The rest of us will wait right here."

"Now just how in the hell would I find him without getting shot? Somebody is bound to see us when we ride off. They could foller us right here."

"Damn it Buck! Yer not an idiot! Y'all just ride into town all easy like and hit the saloon. Find the town drunk and feed him a little whiskey. Take yore time, don't get pushy. You grab that gun maker when nobody is looking."

"I don't know, sounds awful risky to me."

"You want'a go back and face J R without that rifle er

136

take him the feller that can make him a gob of um? He'll blow our damn heads clean off."

"What the hell. All right, come on Clyde. We'll ride as long as we can sit a saddle then stop an get a little rest."

Just as the sun broke the horizon, they were ten miles north of Las Cruces, under large cottonwood trees sound asleep. Shorty, David and Leo, with breakfast over, were watching eight tired saddled horses standing in front of the bar.

"Damn, those idiots left those horses standing all night."

Shorty was leaned against the corner of the hardware store and said, "Yeah, but we're looking at eight horses. Two of um must have rode out sometime last night."

"Think they went back to El Paso?" Leo looked at David then over to Shorty.

"Yeah I'd say so. They must have gone back to let J R know they hadn't caught me yet."

"Think these fellers will go on to Chloride looking for me?"

"That'd be my guess. We'll just have to wait an see."

* * * *

Mister Goss handed Dick a letter. "Now Dick, you tell Curly we have ten days getting those cattle over to the railroad. Also tell him I have cars ordered, but it'll take five er six days for enough trains to come through where they can haul that many cars. He'll know how to handle it. I'll be over about the same time y'all arrive with the herd."

Dick and Albert headed out in a long lope. Albert thought a minute then said, "I'll bet you can hardly wait to get there so you can eat some really good grub. Yep that Nell girl is quite the cook. Uh huh, oh yeah."

Dick never said a word, but Nell was strong on his mind. They made north camp right at noon, just in time for dinner. As they rode up to the barn, the few cowboys that were there waited until horses were taken care of. They were all glad to see both Dick and Albert. Rick asked, "What'er ya'll doing back so soon?"

"Got a letter here for Curly."

"And it took both of you to bring it?" He smiled, slapping Dick on the back.

As they walked inside, Nell turned from the stove with a pot of beans and darn near dropped them at seeing Dick. She glanced at her father then back at Dick. "Y'all pull up a chair, everything is on the table." She quickly sat down and motioned for Dick to sit beside her.

As Dick said howdy to everyone, he handed Curly the letter. They all helped themselves to food, passing platter after bowl, after platter around the table. After a swig of coffee and with a mouth full of food, Curly opened and read the letter.

"Darn, wonder why we didn't just do this when we had all them cattle rounded up. Times gonna be short, we'll start soon's we finish eating."

"Curly, Mister Goss said something about this sale of these beefs being a special order from the Government in Philadelphia. They're shipping um to some island where they're gonna start raising cattle for milk an food."

"Some island, well I'll be dogged. We'll have to make sure every head is in good shape. It didn't say in the letter, but I'll run in a good bull with every fifty er so head of cows."

As they talked and ate their food, no one noticed Nell's left hand on Dick's right knee. He sure knew it was there, as several times he darn near stuttered as he talked.

Over the next five days cattle were rounded up, with young cows and bulls cut from the bunch and guarded night and day where they could not mix back in with the main herd. Albert rode up close to Curly and said, "Them last twenty-two head makes the count three thousand an four head."

"Alright, get the boys and head them others back out to pasture. Be sure and get back before supper. Oh, how many boys did Dick keep watching the shippers?"

"Including Dick there's eight of um."

"That'll do. Y'all go ahead and get them cattle gone and get back an eat. We'll have to have night guards switched off ever three hours. Six to nine then nine to midnight. Well go ahead, I'll pick out the boys that I'm not taking on the drive and they can stand last watch from midnight till we pull out in the morning."

Curly rode on to the barn and unsaddled his horse. Walking inside the cook shack, he asked Nell if they had enough food in the store room to supply the chuck wagon."

"Yeah but you'll sure have to bring enough back from Rifle to re-stock us. It's sure gonna leave us low. How many men are you leaving here?"

"Four is all I can spare. I'm taking sixteen along so we can ride night guard as well as drive that herd."

"Then I'm going along as cook?"

"Now just who do you think I'd take? If Tubby did the cooking ever hand I've got would ride off and never come back. You know a person could throw one of his biscuits through a barn wall. It's still middle afternoon, I'd best go out there and get a couple of the boys busy loading the chuck wagon."

"No! They can help me, but I have to know where things are put or nobody would ever get to eat."

Curly went back to the barn and saddled his horse then rode out to the herd. Circling around, it was a few minutes before he rode up to Dick. "Dick, I think six boys can handle this herd the rest of the day. I need you to pick out a hand and go help Nell load the chuck wagon. Be sure both water barrels are full. That'll be plenty even if the creek is running clear."

Dick unwound his right leg from around the saddle

horn and asked, "How long will it take us getting this herd to the rail head?"

"Three days at the most, two and a half if we're lucky."

Curly went ahead riding around the herd telling the other men Dick and Ed were gone to load the chuck wagon. The first thing Dick and Ed did was take care of the horses, then start cleaning the chuck wagon.

Nell called out the door, "Dick, I'll need y'all to start carrying out a sack of flour and one of corn meal. Just make sure all those pots and pans are washed before re-hanging them in the wagon."

Ed said, "Dick, you go ahead and get the stuff she wants brought along. I'll start on these pots and pans."

As Dick stepped inside the shack, Nell grabbed and held him in a long sweet kiss. When they let go of one another, Nell smiled, "Darn but I've needed that. You do know I'm going along as cook."

"Naw! Darn that's great! You know Nell, while I's at headquarters, I missed you so darn much I wanted to ride all this way just to see you."

"Why didn't you?"

"It would have took all night here and back. All I'd got to done is kiss you one time fore heading back."

She smiled, "Even one kiss would have helped."

She walked with him to the store room for the flour. He saw it was the last bag except for maybe a half that was setting to one side. "We gonna get supplies in Rifle?"

"Yeah, Dad said we'd be there maybe three er four day er more. I figger the day before we head back we'll take the wagon around and load up with a couple months supply. Oh, you go ahead and also take a sack of those pinto beans. I've got to finish fixing supper." She kissed him one more time and just turned back to the kitchen when in walked Curly.

He saw her and asked, "Dick need help back there?"

"Yeah maggin so, he's still got beans, flour, and corn

meal ... Oh darn I almost forgot. Be sure and take along that gallon bucket of lard or we won't have biscuits, steak or very little else. And Dad, when the fellers ride in, could you have um bring in the eggs? I want to take eight er ten dozen along. I've got around seven dozen more than it'll take for breakfast."

"Honey, yer gonna have to start keeping a list of what you want took on the chuck wagon."

"Why? We only use it twice a year, except for this year."

Curly laughed, "Yer right, if we forget anything we'll just do without. How's supper coming along?"

"It'll be ready on time."

Dick was making his second trip when Curly handed him the gallon of hog lard. "The water barrels filled yet?"

"That's next. Ed just got through washing and drying the pots and pans and is washing out the barrels right now."

"Well I'll be darned! You mean I won't have to drink coffee with sand and grit in it!"

"When'd you ever do that? I mean other than what blows in it from a dust storm."

"We don't have dust storms up here. A little sand once in awhile is all, but ever darn time Tubby was our cook, he never looked to see how much dirt and sand was in them water barrels before filling them."

Dick and Ed just finished loading the wagon as the other cowboys stared riding up to the lot and unsaddling their horses. Albert called over, "Hey Dick, any idea who's gonna be left here?"

"Nope, no idea, but I know after supper them six boys at the herd has to be relived so they can come on in an eat."

Curly stepped out the door and hollered for everyone to come on to supper. "Oh, grab all the eggs you can find an bring um in."

CHAPTER TWELVE

Buck and Clyde rode into Chloride late on the second evening. "Clyde, we've gotta hay and grain these horses er they won't be worth a damn." They rode straight to the livery where Bud Beal asked if they wanted to stall their horses.

"Yeah and hay and grain um right good. They've been rode a fair piece. Which one of them saloons has the best whiskey an women?"

"I'd have to say the Burnt Mine. Store bought whiskey and nice gals that don't rob you."

"Thanks, we'll pick our horses up sometime tomorrow."

"If yer wanting to eat a bite, Bill and Kathy's café throws out the best grub in town."

"Thanks, we'll stop off there first."

After one of the best meals they ever had, they walked across and down the street to the Burnt Mine Saloon. A piano was plunking away and a woman singing way off key, but it didn't seen to bother all the drunks.

Bellying up to the bar, Buck called for whiskey. The bartender smiled and asked, "Shot er bottle?"

"Bottle." They took the bottle and two glasses and headed for a table close to the stairway. Here they could see all the girls as they took men up and later back down laughing and carrying on.

As the evening turned to night, they hadn't seen no town drunk yet. Clyde said he was going to get his self a woman and would be back down after a bit. He headed upstairs with a large, plump gal on his arm, just as the sheriff walked in. Stopping at the bar, Sheriff Dobbs ordered a beer, this got Buck's attention in a heart beat.

As Dobbs looked around the room, Buck kept his eyes on his glass of whiskey. He didn't know if this sheriff had posters out on him or not. He reached down and slowly removed the tie down to his forty-four.

Ten minutes later, the sheriff walked out, letting Buck breath a bit easier. Down the stairs walked Clyde and the plump woman with Clyde asking her if she would like to sit with him for awhile.

"Thank you, but my boss wouldn't like that. If you are here for awhile, I'll see if I can break free."

"You do that Honey. I'll be settin' right here."

As he dropped into a chair he told Buck he should try some of that. "She's right friendly."

"Hell they all are as long as you've got money! You see that wobbly feller at the bar? I've been watching him a bit. When nobody was looking, he'd reach and grab somebody else's drink and down it in one swallow. Now I'd say that is our town drunk."

"How er we gonna get him over here without drawing attention? Course there ain't nobody standing right close."

"Walk over and ask him if he'd want to help us finish off this bottle, being as we can't stay all that long."

Clyde eased up to the bar and stood beside the drunk, who was looking around to see if there was a drink he could grab. "Hey feller, would you mind coming over to my table and helping me and my partner finish off a good bottle of whiskey?"

Through blood shot eyes he stammered, "Yer offering to buy me a drink?" He couldn't believe his ears.

"Yes I shor am. Me and my partner bought a whole bottle and it's more'n we can drink. We could stand a little help."

"Then just for you Mister, I'll do er."

They made their way through miners and town workers

and Clyde held out a chair, which the drunk readily took. As they sit down, Buck smiled and poured three glasses full. With a smile on his face, the drunk slowly picked up his glass and sniffed. "Yep, that's good whiskey. He downed it in one gulp and as his glass hit the table, Buck refilled it.

"It looks like you have yore self quite a thirst there feller."

"Yeah, shor do. I don't get to drink nigh as must as I use to. Friends of mine, people I've knowed a long time are getting so dad blasted tight they won't even buy a feller in need a drink much any more. It's a shame friends will treat a feller that way."

"Well we've got to get our selves a room here after a bit. We have to pull out early in the morning. We just came into town to see that feller that made that odd looking rifle. Just hadn't been able to find him."

Another round was poured as the drunk said, "Did you look in the livery? Owns that livery he does. Made that gun for a friend of his. Now that's what I call a friend. If he's my friend I'd bet he'd buy me a drink anytime I needed one."

Buck looked over at Clyde and smiled. "Well feller, we've gotta get, but you go right ahead and finish off that bottle."

"You'd better tell Manny. He see me with this bottle he'll think I stole it and'll throw my butt out in the street."

"Who's Manny?"

"The bartender."

Clyde and Buck stopped by the bar on their way out and told Manny they had left their bottle with that fellow over there nursing it. Manny laughed, "That ought'a hold him the rest of the night. He's a harmless ol' coot, but bothers paying customers."

Buck stopped on the walkway and looked down the street toward the sheriff's office. No light was seen shining from any window. "We're pulling out now. I just wished we'd thought of trail grub. We'll ride through Winston in the morning and get some."

They got to the livery just as Bud was fixing to blow out the lanterns. "Y'all riding tonight?"

"Yeah, and saddle a third horse."

"A third horse, why?"

"Yer coming with us."

"Me! Why me? Where are we going?"

"You'll find out, now get that horse saddled!"

Fifteen minutes later, they rode east by northeast headed for Winston. "We're gonna camp fer the night out here a few miles. You cause us any trouble an it'll be the last trouble you cause anybody. We're tying you up while we get some shut eye."

An hour later they were all fast asleep, with Bud wondering what in the hell was going on. He kept asking them why they grabbed him and where were they taking him. "Shut yore mouth an keep it shut and you just might get there alive."

At this same moment, Shorty, David and Leo had them a hotel room and were about to get some sleep.

Leo said, "Well Shorty, it's been two days and they hadn't moved out'a that bar except to take the horses to the livery. What in the hell do you suppose their waiting on?"

"No idea, unless they're waiting on the two that went back to El Paso. They should have the sense to know they've lost me for good. They must really be going to Chloride to get you and are just waiting word from J R. Somehow we'll have to stop um, even if we have to bushwhack the whole lot."

David asked, "How long are we gonna wait?"

"As long as it takes, these hombres are too dog gone dangerous not to be stopped. I'll probably even have to go back and get J R before this is done."

One hour after sunup, a woman pulled a wagon to a

stop in front of the sheriff's office. Walking inside, Sheriff Dobbs looked up with a surprised look on his face. "Betsy Beal, what are you doing in town this early?"

"Have you see Bud?"

"Not since yesterday evening late. "Why, didn't he come home last night?"

"No and his saddle and horse are not in the livery. Now you know he'd not just ride off an leave me an the kids. Something has had to happen to him."

"Maybe he... Well I can't think of anything he would do cept go home. I'll go to the livery and see if I can make anything out of this. You go on back home to the kids and when I find out anything I'll let you know."

"Now Sheriff, you know he's not a drinking man. He's been off booze since the last baby was born, four years now."

"I know that Betsy, I'll find him. Don't you worry, that'd do no good at all."

"Well I am worried, something is darn shor wrong."

Sheriff Dobbs went to the livery and looked all around. There was no sign of a struggle. He headed toward the first saloon. *'By dogged for Betsy and the kids sake, I shor hope he's not hitting the bottle again.'*

Saloon after saloon he asked if they had seen Bud Beal, no one had. With two more saloons to go, he stopped in the Burnt Mine and walked up to the bar. "Manny, Bud Beal wasn't in here last night, was he?"

"Naw, I hadn't seen him go into no saloon in years."

"How about any strangers?"

"Naw I can't say... Wait a minute! Yeah there was two strangers at that table right over yonder. Why I remember is when they left, they give Carl Rogers over half a bottle of damn good drinking whisky. Seemed like friendly fellers."

"Wouldn't happen to know where I could find Carl this time of morning?"

"Yeah, he's sleeping it off in my shed right out back."

Sheriff Dobbs went out the back door and banged right loud on a flimsy shed door. "Carl! You in there?"

"Yeah, go away I need my sleep."

"Carl, this is Sheriff Dobbs and I need to talk to you."

"Would you buy me coffee and breakfast?"

"I guess so. Come on and we'll go over to Kathy and Bill's."

Twenty minutes later they were drinking coffee and Carl was eating a good meal. Carl looked up after putting a fork full of scrambled eggs into his mouth. "Now what in the world would you want to be talking to me about, Sheriff?"

"Last night in the Burnt Mine, two men left you with nigh on to a full bottle of whiskey."

"Yes Sir they shor did. Good whiskey, it was."

"What all did y'all talk about"

"They was in town only for a short time an wanted to talk to the feller what made that funny looking rifle. I told um to ask at the livery. So they upped and left me the bottle when they walked out. Said they was going to bed."

"Didn't you know the U S Marshal, David and Leo have gone after the rifle? It was stolen over a week ago."

"No, I never heared nothing like that. Why, is something wrong, Sheriff?"

"Yes, it's looking like they took Bud Beal with them."

"Why'd they go an do a thing like that?"

"I'd say they might think it was Bud that made that rifle."

"What'er you gonna do?"

"I have no idea. Wait until the marshal gets back, I guess."

* * * *

The cattle drive to Rifle went very well and the herd

Paul L. Thompson

was bedded down less than a half day's push from the rail-road. As everyone ate supper and drank coffee, Curly said he was proud of every one of them. "I've gotta let y'all know, yer the best bunch of cowboy drovers I've ever had. We'll make Rifle well fore noon tomorrow. I'd guess Mister Goss and the ramrod will be waiting.

"Now I don't want none of y'all hitting no saloon an twisting off till ever one of these cows are on that train and gone. Then I'll give you two days on the town."

Breakfast was early and the drive was on the way before the sun was up. Dick got to stay and help Nell put everything away in the wagon and get it ready to roll. She would be bringing up the rear, just far enough back to stay out of the dust. As Dick started to ride off she called out, "You'll go for a walk along the creek with me tonight after supper, won't you?"

He hollered, "Wouldn't miss it!"

Mister Goss and his ramrod saw the trail dust and rode out to meet the herd. When he saw the cows and bulls, he told the ramrod, "What did I tell you? Curly knew exactly which cattle to bring. I'd forgot to tell him in my letter about bringing any bulls. These all look to be two and three year olds, strong and healthy."

Jacob looked over at Mister Goss asking, "Are you really going to give all these boys a twenty dollar bonus?"

"I most certainly am, except for Curly, his will be fifty. The job they did was well worth it. It's hard to find good hands that work for the brand no matter how many hours a day they work."

Jacob smiled as he said, "Boss, I've got in mind being around their camp come supper time. That daughter of Curly's is the best dog gone little cook I've ever had the pleasure of sitting at the same table with."

"Well if it's that good, we'll both stay."

Jacob spotted Curly, so they rode around the on coming herd where they met and talked. "Looks like you'll make that pond well before dinner time."

"Yes Sir, that's what I was hoping. I'm gonna have Nell set up the chuck wagon around to the southwest side among them big ol' trees. While the cattle drink, I'll have a couple of the boys help her so she can get dinner on. Have the rail cars got here yet?"

Mister Goss looked back toward the rail siding and loading dock, though it was too far to see anything. "Yes, but only twelve of them so far. The station master said more would be coming in by noon tomorrow. We have to have these loaded where that train can hook on to um, so that side rail will hold the next bunch. The first car is lined up with the loading dock now."

"Then we'll get these cattle into the loading pens and start loading right after breakfast in the morning. We ought'a have that done well before that train gets here."

"If the railroad pays me any mind, day after tomorrow's train will have two engines with enough cars to finish taking the whole bunch. If not, it could dribble out for over a week." Mister Goss had sent a wire to the railroad headquarters telling them these cattle were for the Government and would have to be fed and watered at least twice before reaching Philadelphia. "They had better pay heed to that or they'll have dead or sick cows."

"If an idiot didn't get the wire, they'll do it."

The chuck wagon was set up and a few cowboys at a time came in and ate dinner, while others circled the herd to keep them from wondering off too far looking for grass.

An hour before sundown, word was spread that supper was ready. Curly, Mister Goss and Jacob were first in line, as cowboys' unsaddled horses and grabbed a plate. Nell had cooked a very big pot of pinto beans, biscuits and steak.

They all sat around feeding their faces and Jacob could tell Mister Goss was impressed with what he was eating.

After the meal was over, cowboys got up to go out and relieve the other boys so they could ride in and eat.

Mister Goss placed his empty plate and coffee cup on the wagon tail gate. "Nell, after eating your cooking, I can see why no hand has dragged up from north camp. I might just take you back to headquarters with me." He smiled right big.

"Thank you Sir, I do my best."

He started to walk off but turned back, "Are you married?"

"Oh no Sir, I'm surly not."

"Got a boyfriend?"

"Nell quickly looked at her father, then over at Dick."

"Might, but does it matter?"

"Naw, no it sure doesn't. I just didn't want to think I'd be losing the best cook we've ever had anytime soon." He turned toward Curly and winked and got a smile in return.

After supper dishes were washed and everything put away, a fresh pot of coffee was left where it would stay warm above the fire. Dick gave Nell a hand up behind his saddle, just as Curly rode back in. "Where are y'all off to?"

Nell quickly said, "We're gonna take a walk along the creek. You know I do every time we come to town."

Curley smiled to himself, "That's mighty fine, it'll keep Dick away from all them saloon girls."

"Pop! He don't do that no way."

"How do you know?"

"I just do, that's all."

"Well don't be gone all that long, morning will come early."

When they got out of sight, Nell put her arms around Dick's waist and laid her head on his shoulder. "Dick, we've gotta do something, and I mean really quick."

"We are doing something, we're going to walk by the river."

"No silly, I mean where we can be together more. I want you to hold me so bad sometimes I could scream."

"Yeah I know, but there's always too many of the boys around fer us to do that. And when we get back to camp I'll most likely have to go back over to headquarters."

"Then I'll ask Mister Goss if he really meant it when he said he'd like me over there."

"What'll Curly say?"

"Oh darn it I don't know! All I know is I want to be with you all the time. Why don't you just marry me?"

"Okay."

"Okay! You mean you will!"

"Sure, if Curly will let me."

She jerked his head around and kissed him right on the lips. They dismounted at the creek and Dick tied the horse then pulled Nell into his arms. "Let's not stay here too long an go back an ask him tonight when we get back to camp. We hurry maybe he won't be asleep yet."

"Alright, but you leave your horse saddled just incase he wants to shoot you and you have to run."

"You think he would!"

"No silly, I was just joshing."

Dick pulled away and placed his hands on her shoulders. She looked at him with a puzzled look. "What's wrong?" She thought he was about to back out on marrying her.

"Nell, I love you more than anything in the whole world, but I've got to tell you some things about me."

"No you don't! You said you loved me, that's all I need to know, because I've waited all my life for you."

"Nell I have to let you know. The reason me an Albert are in Colorado, is we got into some trouble down in New Mexico Territory. I just want you to know."

"Did you kill anybody?"

"No, heck no!"

"Then don't say another word, it is over and done with. You are here with me now, that's all that matters. You never have to go back there. Now come on, let's go talk to Pop."

Dick mounted then removed his left boot from the stirrup and gave Nell a hand up behind the saddle. She was so happy she wanted to scream to the world she was going to marry her feller.

"Oh Dick I can hardly wait. If Pop says it's alright, let's look up the preacher and get married tonight."

"Tonight! Naw we'd better wait till all these cattle are shipped. Curly said he'd give ever body a couple of days in town fore we have to start back."

"Okay, just don't you forget."

He laughed then leaned back and kissed her. Riding in, they stopped and dismounted at the tag line and walked over by the fire where Curly and a couple men were drinking coffee.

As they walked up Curly said, "That wadn't long, get into some kind of argument?" He smiled as Nell reached and held Dick's left hand. Dick was so nervous he had to clear his throat before talking. "Curly, I'm needing to ask you if it'd be alright if me an Nell got married."

He quickly stood, staring at both young people. With his hands on hips, he saw Dick was about to run, so he spoke fast. "It's darn shor about time! I was beginning to think I was gonna have to ask her for you. Now when's this gonna happen?" The grin on his face told Nell she had picked the right man.

She let go of Dick's hand and threw her arms around her father's neck. "Oh Pop, you know I love you so much. Thank you, we'll both make you proud."

"I already am. Yer two fine kids that need each other, now y'all go on and make yore plans, I'm hitting my bedroll."

CHAPTER THIRTEEN

Buck and Clyde got Bud to Las Cruces late in the evening two days later. They tied up in front of the saloon while looking all around. As they dismounted Clyde asked, "Wonder where Neil an nem are? I don't see a one of their horses."

Buck looked over at him as if he were an idiot. "Damn it Clyde, they wadn't gonna leave them horses tied here to no hitch rail fer four er five days. They said they'd be here."

As they walked in, Neil was one of the first to see them. He stood and waited until they got close enough to talk without hollering. "Damn, you got him! Y'all go ahead and get a drink. Gene, you and the rest of the boys go get our horses saddled. We'll be at the livery in a quarter hour."

"You mean we're pulling out tonight!"

"Hell yes, tonight! Now get!"

Bud stood there, not understanding why these men grabbed him and what they were going to do with him. As they all sat for a drink, he had figured out Neil must be the boss. As the whiskey bottle was emptied he asked, "Feller, why in the hell did y'all grab me? I don't got no money, I'm just a small farmer. I've got a hundred and twenty acres, a wife and four kids."

Buck took the glass from his lips saying, "Yeah and you also own a livery and make new rifles."

"Me! Own the livery! Make rifles! Mister you've got it all wrong. I was just caring for the livery for Leo while him an David and U S Marshal Shorty Thompson went looking for a rifle what was stole by a couple of Mexicans."

Buck looked over at Neil then back at Bud before saying, "Now Neil, me an Clyde both was told the man that made that rifle was in the livery. We went an got him."

Bud laughed right out loud. "Mister you've got the wrong man. I can't even repair my own plows much less make a rifle. On top of that, I've never even seen the rifle. Heard about it, but never seen it. Leo got me to watch the place till he gets back. Right about now my wife has Sheriff Dobbs out looking for me."

Neil sat there damn near blowing steam out of both ears. "Mister if yer lying…"

"I ain't lying. If you read the paper, it told the name of the young feller what owns that rifle. My name is Bud Beal. That's farmer Bud Beal and the only rifle I own is ten years old."

"Well son of ah… Damn it we've gotta come up with something. Wait a minute! You said three men came after that rifle, why did we see only one?"

Bud asked, "What'd he look like?"

"A young cowboy, maybe twenty-five er so."

"That'd be U S Marshal Thompson. Leo is around nineteen an David is seventeen going on eighteen. They'll get that rifle. That U S Marshal is suppose to be the best gun anywhere around."

"Yeah I believe that. We saw some of his shooting. Buck, see what's holding the boys. We need to get on the road."

"What if that marshal is right here in Las Cruces?"

Neil quickly looked all around, stood up and said, "Let's ride, damn it now!" A cold chill just ran down his spine.

Bud sat there and asked, "What about me? Can I go on back home?"

"Hell no! We might need you to back off that marshal."

Clyde threw the last drop of whiskey down his throat saying. "We couldn't out run a fat milk cow on them tired horses of ours. How in the hell can we out run some marshal?"

154

"Leaving at night, maybe they won't know which way we went. We can make El Paso by noon tomorrow." Neil was thinking, hard. "Yeah, maybe he ain't no where around no way. We ain't seen hide nor hair of him in damn near a week."

They hit their saddles and took the stage road south. Shorty, Leo and David sat finishing supper and drinking one last cup of coffee. "Leo, I want you an David to go over to that saloon and check on the boys. Count um an make sure there's still only eight. I'll be down the street at the Desert Saloon."

David asked, "Why do you think they're still here? Them other two have had plenty of time to make it to and back from El Paso at least twice."

"No idea, but I'm thinking they'll still go to Chloride after you. They ain't done trying for that rifle."

Shorty paid for their meals and headed for the saloon down the street. David and Leo walked into the bar and looked all around, not seeing the men. Leo asked the bartender if he knew when they left. "Yep, a little over a half hour ago three more came in and they had a few drinks. Some left right away then ten er fifteen minutes later the others left."

"Thanks feller."

He and David hot footed it to find Shorty. When told, all Shorty could think of to say was, damn. "Now where in the hell would they be riding at night? Now maybe they got word about something er could'a spotted me and are trying to throw anybody off their trail. Let's head for the livery."

As they walked in the hostler asked, "Y'all riding at night too?" In the dim lantern light, he looked at Shorty.

"Naw we'll wait till morning, but did you happen to hear where them hombres were headed?"

"Naw not really, but the way I took it, it was to El Paso."

Shorty thought a minute then asked, "Had you seen um all before?"

"Naw, not the three of um on tired horses. One of them said the long ride from Chloride was awful hard on their horses."

"Chloride!"

"Yep, that's what he said alright."

"Are for sure he didn't say the ride to Chloride would be hard on the horses?"

"Shor I'm shor. To and from are completely different words. He said from. Yeah and them three horses was already give plumb out. They won't make too many more miles fore they quit."

"What time do you open in the morning?"

"Five-o-clock. I have to get the stage horses fed and watered so they'll be done before they are hooked to the stage."

"We'll be here right after breakfast."

They started to walk off when the hostler said, "Oh Marshal, there was one thing I thought was mighty strange."

"Yeah, what's that?"

"One of the fellers was dressed just like a farmer and was the only one not wearing a gun."

Leo said, "Shorty, you don't suppose them two went to Chloride and grabbed Bud, thinking it was me. Naw, surly they wouldn't ah done that."

"By jacks that's what it's starting to sound like. I don't think they'd hurt him none though, he don't know nothing."

"Yeah but they might not know that and think he's lying."

Shorty shook his head. "Well I'll tell you boys one thing, that dad gummed rifle sure has caused a lot of trouble. We'll head for El Paso in the morning and see if they're taking him to J R. Yeah, come to think on it, we'll go by train an beat um there. Steve, we won't be taking our horses in the morning after all. Just keep um fed and watered while we're gone."

156

* * * *

Dick and Nell waited to be married until all the cattle shipped. That way all the cowboys and Mister Goss could attend the wedding. Sheriff Young, his wife and baby Dick along with sister-in-law Rachel sat in the front row.

The small church was full, but Albert got to sit beside Rachel, who kept smiling and asking why he hadn't been back over to see her. "We've been working cattle pretty much, but when they said we was gonna ship a bunch, I knew I'd somehow get to see you while I's in town." She lowered her eyes then looked straight at him. He blushed while looking into those beautiful eyes.

"Do you think you can get away for awhile around sundown?"

"Sure, the cattle are shipped an we have two days on the town. Why at sundown?"

"I thought maybe you would like to go for a walk along the creek. It sure is pretty in late evening."

"There's nothing I'd like better. Do you want me to come by your house?"

"Yes, its best Ron and Mary know who I am with. I've never taken a walk with anyone before, it's always been alone."

The wedding was over and the local women had tables set up under large shade trees. Dinner was about ready. As everyone walked out of the church, loud clapping and shouts were heard from all the cowboys then the town's people joined in.

Ron led Nell and Dick to a table with a very pretty cloth all spread out. On the table were presents from cowboys, the Young family and even Mister Goss. Curly had to give a short speech.

"Ever body get a glass of punch, I want to make a toast."

Glasses were filled then came the quiet. Curly cleared his throat and said, "This toast is to a new beginning for my beautiful daughter Nell, and my new son-in-law Dick. He not only got a pretty wife, he got the best darn cook in Colorado. Now let's eat and visit awhile."

Mister Goss eased over and handed Dick a small envelope. "Son, Curly has told me you and your brother are darn good hands. I'm proud to have you working for me. Enjoy your new married life, and keep up the good work."

Dick started to open the envelope, but Mister Goss said, "No Son. You wait until y'all are in your room at the hotel to open that."

The meal was over around two-o-clock and most of the cowboys had wondered off to the saloon. Dick and Nell were seen going into the hotel while Curly and Mister Goss thought it time to go have a drink.

Albert got to walk Rachel home, along with Ron and Mary. Just before stepping upon the porch Rachel asked, "Albert, what do you think of Dick and Nell marrying?"

He smiled as he looked at Ron first. "Well I have to say along with the best brother in the world, I now have a sister that will keep him from ever being lonely again. I don't think he could'a married a sweeter woman."

Mary said she needed to go on inside and put the baby down for his nap. "Ron honey, you come along to. I might need some help." She winked where Rachel nor Albert saw it.

"Huh, oh yeah. Rachel, why don't you an Albert stay out here on the porch for awhile? We wouldn't want y'all laughing and waking the baby."

They sat on the swing, slowly rocking back and forth. Rachel looked toward the door then reached over and took Albert's hand. "It's middle afternoon, why don't I go in and tell Ron and Mary we're going for a walk down on the creek?"

"Yeah, that'd be great. It'll give us more time together."

Dick and Nell walked into their room, placing the gifts on the bed. He took her in his arms, kissing her deeply. "Well Mrs. Boggs, now that you are a married woman, are you happy?"

"Oh yes, this is the happiest day of my life."

"Then let's open these presents and see what we got."

Dick got a new shirt and two neckerchiefs along with four pair of socks. Nell was so surprised to see a new dress her father had gotten her. Mary had given her a breast cloth and two pair of right pretty bloomers. She blushed as she held them up for Dick to see. "Will you look at these!"

Dick reached in his pocket, "Oh, I most forgot this envelope from Mister Goss." He carefully opened it and Nell watched as his eyes got big. "Look Nell! A hundred and twenty dollars! Darn that's three months pay."

"What are we gonna do with it? You know everything we need, Mister Goss furnishes."

"We'll start our own bank account. I even have a dab of money saved up. I'll just put it all in there. If we both save our money, in a few years maybe we can buy us a small place."

"I would sure like that and when Pop gets too old to work any more, he can come live with us. Oh, and Albert too."

"I'm thinking Albert will have his own wife for too awful long. At the wedding, him and Rachel was eye balling each other pretty dog gone good."

* * * *

Shorty, Leo and David made it to El Paso by eight-o-clock that morning. Neil and his bunch with Bud along hadn't made twenty miles and had another twenty-five or so to go. They had camped for the night about ten miles south of Las Cruces. Three of the horses had been so tired they were stumbling. This morning all was well and they were moving right along.

Neil was rolling over in his mind what he was going to tell J R. He knew it would be bad, but he'll tell that little cowboy is a U S Marshal. He'll say he was worried the marshal might find out about J R's gun running deal. He might even bring in the cavalry, being as the most guns they sold were stolen from them. He might even want to kill this farmer just to keep him quiet.

'Yeah, J R might even want to go to Mexico for awhile.'

Buck was riding close and asked, "What'd you say?"

"I'm thinking with a U S Marshal nosing around, all our asses could be in trouble. Mexico is looking better to me every minute."

Clyde heard that and said, "Yeah, and all over a worthless piece of crap rifle we didn't even get."

Stepping from the train, Shorty led the way as they walked toward the sheriff's office. Leo looked over at David, but spoke to Shorty. "I thought you said you didn't want local law involved in this. Now yer gonna go tell um what we're gonna do."

"Yeah, the law will find out when lead starts to fly anyhow, and I don't want um shooting at us."

The sheriff's office was about six blocks north of J R's gun shop, so Shorty wasn't too worried about being seen. He had no idea how many more men he might have.

Walking into the office, there sat two fat, sloppy looking Spaniards, or maybe even Mexicans. They were dressed like Mexican Army, with the large sombreros, tight pants with Conchos streaming down both legs. They also wore large spurs and were smoking stinking cigars.

"Howdy, I'm looking for the sheriff." Shorty hesitated telling he was a U S Marshal.

"I am so sorry *Señor,* but our sheriff went and got his self killed no more than a week ago. May we be of service?"

"Naw I don't reckon so. I just wanted to say howdy being as I hadn't been down this'a way in a good while. How did it happen? You know, how'd he die?"

"With a very large bullet between his shoulder blades. Yes it was quite sudden that this happens."

"Well thanks for your information." As they turned and started to walk out Shorty asked, "Are you now the law?"

"Yes, you could say that."

"Thanks again." Shorty motioned with his head for David and Leo to follow him up the street, away from J R's.

"What do you think Shorty?"

"No idea, but I've gotta find somebody and see what they think of their new law. Maybe we'll step into one of these businesses and ask."

Before he did that, Shorty pointed at a church steeple and slowly looked back toward the sheriff's office. One of the fat Mexicans was standing in the doorway watching their every move.

"Just keep walking and sight seeing. We have eye balls on our backs. Here, let's take this street and head… Wait, there's the livery where we left our horses last time we was here. Maybe that feller will talk. He seemed friendly enough."

They rounded the corner and were out of sight of the sheriff's office. Another half block and they were at the livery. The hostler was driving a nail in a two by four where he was going to hang a bucket. Shorty said howdy.

"Howdy fellers, when y'all left here the other day, I wasn't expecting you back. Where's yore horses?"

"Left um in Las Cruces and came down on the train. I was needing to see Sheriff Holman." Shorty had no idea who the sheriff was. He was just feeling this fellow out to see which side he was on.

"Who?"

"Sheriff Holman."

"Never heard of him. Our sheriff was Calvin Gipson."

"You say was, what happened to him, quit?"

"Hell no he didn't quit! That damned Carlson and his gang of Mexicans shot him in the back. Shot him right about where yer standing, just as he started to dismount."

"Who is Carlson?"

"J R Carlson, the biggest killer and crook this side of Mexico. Hell that's where he ought'a be, Mexico."

"When did all that happen?"

"The next day after y'all left here."

"Shit fire, don't y'all have a mayor and city fathers?"

"Yeah an they're too damn scared to even go take a crap by their selves. Everybody in this town is buffaloed. I tried getting some men together, but ever one of um had something else to do. I'm thinking of riding to the fort and get the cavalry. Somebody has to do something er there won't be a town left. J R has give a bunch of Mexicans free run of everything. They go drink, they don't pay. They stall a horse, they don't pay. This can't go on."

"You know he has a bunch of men that ain't Mexican."

"Yeah, but half of um rode out before you did and ain't been back. Maybe they're scared of them Mexicans."

"Naw, they're riding this'a way right now and should be here in about two er three hours."

"Damn that's all I need. I'm damn near out of feed now, but I damn shor ain't gonna buy more just to feed their damn horses for free. I ought'a stand here and gut shoot ever one of um."

"Naw, that'd get you killed. Do you know of any business men that if they had a leader would stand up and help clean this town? Hell with help we could take J R and all these Mexicans."

"I don't think I could get over two er three. Everybody

has families and businesses. They think doing nothing is better than getting shot. Just who in the hell are you, that'd you'd give a shit about this town?"

"I'm U S Marshal Shorty Thompson. J R sent men all the way to Chloride, New Mexico to get this boy's gun. If I don't get him now, he'll just send more."

"Well Marshal, I'd say yer in for a whole lot of trouble. Now I'm willing to help anyway I can and I have a son and brother that'll lend a hand."

"I think we'll need a hell of a lot more men than just six. I'm gonna ride out to Fort Bliss and talk to the commander. It looks to me like he would have already heard about all this trouble. Hell the fort ain't much over a mile from here."

"Yeah but them army boys ain't allowed to come to town all that much. That commander keeps a pretty close rein on um."

"Why is that? I thought all cavalry men twisted off most of the time when they ain't on duty."

"Yeah, but when four er five of um at a time would come in at night, they didn't show back up at the fort. Just to show you how dumb that commander is, he thinks they deserted. Sheriff Gipson tried telling him they was robbed and killed by Carlson's men and throwed in the Rio Grande."

"David, you and Leo hang out right here at the livery till I get back. Feller, do you have a horse you'd loan me."

"Dad gummed right I do! You just tell that commander he needs to get off his butt and help save this town."

Thirty minutes later, Shorty was at the fort gate, trying to see the commander. "Look feller, here is my badge and papers, now I need to see yore commander."

"Commander Jordon don't talk much to town folk."

"Damn it that's what I'm trying to tell you! I ain't from El Paso I'm from New Mexico and am investigating a gang of outlaws."

The sergeant handed Shorty's badge and papers back to him then turned to a corporal. "Spencer, you stand right here. Marshal, you wait with him while I go talk with General Jordon."

It was a good fifteen minutes before the sergeant was back. "Marshal, you can come on in." As Shorty dismounted and led the horse beside the sergeant, he was looking all around."

"Sergeant, you can correct me if I'm wrong, but you and that corporal seem afraid of the commander."

The sergeant looked at Shorty and smiled, "You will be too, Marshal. He's a smart ass from back east and already knows it all, so don't go trying to tell him how to run the cavalry."

As they walked into the office, the first thing Shorty saw was a pompous ass sitting there like he was a king on a throne. Jordon looked up and said, "Sit down! I only talk to standing men when they are in uniform."

Shorty took a chair and introduced himself. "Yes, Sergeant Jenkins informed me. Now what are you here for?"

"Well General, it looks like a gang of outlaws and Mexicans have taken over El Paso. They have already killed the sheriff and are shaking down all the merchants for weekly payments. There is a gob of um and I could use your help doing it."

"You being a U S Marshal know I can not interfere with the civilian population. It is my duty to keep the Indians under control. That is my soul purpose of being in this God forsaken country. If I were you and needed help, I would wire the Texas Rangers in Austin. I am sure they will lend a hand."

Shorty stood, "General, when I walk out that door it will not be to wire the rangers. I will wire the President. When he made me a U S Marshal, he told me if and when I ran into trouble I couldn't handle, go for the cavalry. Now

I'll bet a month's wages he can get you off your ass and get troops into El Paso."

The General pushed back his chair and bolted to his feet. "Marshal, you will not threaten me! I know my duties!"

"Another thing, when I wire the President, I will also inform him of your missing men. Yes, the ones they went into town and didn't come back. General those men did not desert! They were murdered, robbed and thrown into the Rio Grande. The people of that town know this, why haven't you listened?"

"If that is so, the people did it! I care not what happens to them, I just keep my men out of town so it doesn't happen again."

"Then you are telling me you will not lift a hand to protect the borders of the United States against an invasion from another country! General, El Paso has been invaded by outlaws from Mexico, brought in by a gun runner. Let me ask you this, when was the last time guns and ammunition was missing from your armory? J R Carlson stole them and sold them to Mexican banditos, yes and to the Apache and Comanche."

"And I suppose you have proof of this?"

"Yes I do, his gun shop has more army rifles in it than you have in your armory. I have seen them with my own eyes."

Still standing General Jordon hollered out, "Sergeant Jenkins, at once!"

The sergeant walked in, hat in hand. "Yes Sir, General."

"You will take five men and accompany the marshal into El Paso. You will look the circumstances over and report back to me. I will expect my report within the hour."

"General, you'd better not do that, unless you want to get five men killed. Hell I've got more men that than that and know better than to go against that bunch." Shorty knew this man was dumb.

"Then are you suggesting a full invasion?"

"No Sir, I suggest just the sergeant and I go. Him an me can do more snooping than six cavalrymen on horseback. Another thing, it'll damn shor take longer than an hour."

While Shorty was at the fort, cussing and discussing, David and Leo saw as J R's men rode in from the north. Riding right in the middle was Bud Beal. "Darn it David, they did grab Bud! I shor wish Shorty would get back."

CHAPTER FOURTEEN

When Neil and the boys walked into the gun shop without the rifle, but with a farmer, J R simply lost his mind. "What in the hell are you trying to do to me Neil? I sent you after one little cowboy to get my rifle. What do you do, go an bring back an idiot farmer that wouldn't know a rifle if it hit him in the head.

"When you found out he knowed nothing, why'd you bring him right to me where he can get the law on all of us?"

"That's what I'm trying to tell you J R. That little cowboy is a U S Marshal."

"He's what?"

"Yeah, tell him what you told us." He shoved Bud over in front of J R.

"That's right, U S Marshal Shorty Thompson an two more fellers came looking for that rifle after two Mexkins went an stole it. I'm pretty shor the marshal will get it. From what I hear he's a tough little sucker."

"He already got it and had no trouble doing it! Damn my sorry hide, all I wanted was one stinking rifle that I could copy and maybe make hundreds of. Neil, did y'all see him after he left here? He had to go somewhere."

"Naw, we looked ever where and waited around Las Cruces till Clyde an Buck got back with this farmer. What'er you thinking we ought'a do?"

"What in the hell can we do? That marshal has my rifle and is gone. Maybe he went on back to Chloride and I can take a couple dozen men and still get that rifle back."

Buck said, "Now J R, me an Clyde rode the stage road all the way there an back an never saw him. He didn't go back to Chloride. I'd bet on that, we'd seen him."

167

Neil was worried J R wasn't going to cool down anytime soon. "J R, being as nobody's seen him, you think maybe him an them other two got on the train and is taking that rifle back east to maybe the Winchester Fire Arms Company where they can make a bunch of um? You know, fore somebody went an stole it again er they lost it."

"How in the hell would I know where he went? I've got to get my hands on another thousand rifles by the fifteenth of this month."

Buck looked around, "Hell you've got two er three hundred right here. What do you need that many more for?"

"Them Mexicans are starting a war with their government and will take all the rifles and ammunition I can get um. I already promised um a thousand rifles and fifty thousand rounds of ammunition. It looks like we're gonna to have to get the cavalry away from the fort on a wild goose chase, chasing Indians and hit their armory again."

Neil said, "Wouldn't it be easier hitting Fort Hancock? I know its fifty miles but they don't have nigh as many men as Fort Bliss."

"I think for as many rifles as I need, we'll have to hit um both. I'll get them Mexicans we give the sheriff's job to, to go over to Juarez and bring back three er four dozen men."

Clyde asked. "Want I should turn this farmer loose?"

"Hell no! How stupid can you be? Wait until dark and a couple of y'all take him down to the river and put a bullet in the back of his head."

In about an hour, Shorty and Sergeant Jenkins rode up to the livery. David and Leo both tried talking at once. "Shorty, they got him! Them two men did go to Chloride and grab Bud. We saw um as they rode down the street toward the gun shop. How can we go about getting Bud back without getting him shot?"

"Off hand I'd say that's gonna be tough. Sergeant

Jenkins is here to look things over and see if we can convince the General to send in the cavalry. Stan, you and the sergeant look to be about the same size. Would you have any clothes around here he could wear? Walking into that gun shop in uniform would get him shot."

"Yeah, he can come on over to the house an change. What er you thinking on doing?"

"Being as none of them fellers has seen David an Leo er the sergeant, they'll go into that shop and buy a couple boxes of cartridges. The sergeant can see what I told the General is true. J R has a gob of army rifles in boxes stacked against the back wall."

After a bit, Jenkins, David and Leo walked into the gun shop. There were only five men and one of them was Bud, setting in a far corner with one man close by. He looked up and damn near shouted at Leo, but knew they all would be shot.

As the three walked up to the counter J R asked, "What can I do for you fellers today?"

"Two boxes of .44.40's and one box of .44's." As J R reached and set the boxes on the counter, Bud asked, "Can I write my wife a note and tell her I'll be crossing the river after dark an not to come looking for me. I won't be coming home. Maybe theses fellers right here could mail it for me."

"You can do it later an I'll mail it."

J R looked at him then at the three men at the counter who seemed to be paying no mind to what was said. Leo just paid for the cartridges and asked Jenkins if he needed anything else.

"Naw I don't guess so. I'm needing a new rifle right bad but can't afford one right now."

J R looked up, "I've got some used army rifles I could give you a deal on."

"I don't know, I's leaning toward a new one. What kind'a shape are your used one in?"

"I've got a gob of um an you can take yore pick. Some of um are barely used, worn hardly at all."

"Won't hurt to take a look I don't guess."

J R took him to the back wall and opened a crate of rifles. "Go through um and see if there's one you like."

The fifth rifle he picked up, he said, "Now this un looks right nice." He worked the bolt and sighted down the barrel. "What er you asking?"

"How's thirty dollars sound? Now you know I can get fifty."

Jenkins called over to Leo, "Hey, can you loan me twenty?"

"Shor, but you gotta pay me back come the first."

"Yeah, I can do that."

They bought the rifle, picked up the cartridges and Leo winked at Bud as they left the store. Once outside and a half a block up the street Leo said, "They're gonna kill Bud tonight down by the river."

Jenkins smiled, "Want'a bet? Now let's hot foot it to Shorty."

David asked, "Why'd you buy that rifle? I thought all you had to do was see um."

"Yeah but this rifle belonged to Private Reynolds. He's one of the troopers that the General thinks deserted. If the General don't do something now, Shorty can wire the President and I'll damn shor be a witness against the General."

They made it back to the livery and talked with Shorty and Stan. Shorty looked outside saying, "It's getting late now. We need to be ready down by the river before they bring Bud down. Sergeant, Think you'll need any help convincing the General this town needs his help?"

"Naw, but I'd sure like it if you came to the fort in the morning. You know a hell of a lot more about how to take that bunch then the General or any other officer we have on that post. They'd come riding in here and kill half the town and probably not get a one of the men we want."

The sergeant changed back to his uniform and told them he would see them in the morning. Stan asked, "Shorty, you want me to get my gun and come with y'all to the river?"

"Naw, I don't figger he'll send more than a couple men. I just don't know what in the hell I'm gonna do with them if we don't kill um. That jail has J R's Mexican friends running it. Hell, I'll just throw um all in jail and sit guard myself until I have to go to the fort."

"What'll you do then? Think maybe the General would hold um in his stockade?"

"Might, but I'll just lock the door and take all the keys. Come on David, Leo. We need to get set where we won't be seen before they get Bud to the river. I'd guess they'll bring him the shortest way being as its only a block behind the store."

Just at sundown, they had walked down to the river and Leo spotted a trail leading up to the gun shop. "Damn Shorty, look at this! Bet this is the way they'll come."

"Yep, I'm just glad for all this tall green brush. Heck we can sit two feet from the trail an they can't see us."

David said, "I don't think we'll have to wait all that long. They'll all want to eat supper and hit some saloon fore too long."

Shorty laughed, "Yeah, I just wish it was J R that came, but that won't happen."

It was almost dark, with stars already shining but the moon hadn't come up when they heard voices coming down the trail. One man was saying, "I don't see why J R wants him killed. Hell's fire he's just a farmer and has a family."

The other man said, "Yeah, but family man er not, he could still get us all hung."

Bud was scared, what if David and Leo didn't understand what he was saying. "Fellers, you don't have to kill me. I'll go on back home to my wife an kids an tell nobody nothing. I'll just say I went over to Winston on a drunk."

"I'd like to believe you…" A gun was sticking in the middle of both men's backs. "What… What'da ya want?"

"I want to blow both yore damn heads off but your boss would hear the shots. Now move, up river!"

"Bud said, "Shorty, they was suppose to shoot me in the back of the head and throw me in the river. Don't you think you ought'a fire off one shot so J R will think they went on an done it?"

"Yeah and maybe he'll think they just went on to the bar and are getting drunk when they don't come right back." He fired one shot into the water and herded the two men up river and behind the livery.

"Stan, we got um, but do you know if them Mexicans stay at the jail house this late."

"Yeah but I'd say they are across the street eating supper right about now."

"Alright, then lets get these boys in a cell and wait and see who shows up to join um."

As they were shoved into a cell and the door locked, Shorty informed them if either yelled out and warned anybody, they would be the first shot. "You wouldn't do that! Yer a U S Marshal."

"Mister just you give a yell and my first bullet will get you right between the eyes. Yeah, and you saw how straight I can shoot." David had his rifle in his hands while Leo reached and took a double barreled shot gun off the wall. Checking to make sure it was loaded, he smiled.

"Wouldn't you know, double-ought buck shot. That'll tear anybody in half."

They waited less than twenty minutes when they heard two Mexicans coming, laughing and talking about a young girl they had raped. "I think we should do that again, tonight. She was the best and her mama might be alright also." They walked into the sheriff's office right into three waiting guns.

Shorty spoke with a firm voice, "You make a move for a gun and that shotgun will blow you both back out that door. Now raise yer hands, now!"

Both men looked as it they were trying to catch a flying bird. Their hands shot up while their eyes were looking from gun to gun. "Ah *Señor,* I see's you come's back to check on the dead sheriff. It will do you no good, he is already buried. And tomorrow you will be also. Our *amigos* will be here before noon. There is many of them and you will have no chance."

"David, get their guns, from behind. Don't let one of um try and grab you." David disarmed them, as Shorty pointed toward the cell. "Move, in there with your friends."

After they were locked up Shorty told David and Leo to go ahead and eat, but bring him back a plate. He wasn't going to leave here until he went to the fort.

They were back within forty-five minutes with Shorty a steak, beans, potato and biscuits. "David, you an Leo go ahead and stay with Bud in the livery tonight. You shouldn't be seen up there in the loft. I'll come by for a horse after breakfast. You can meet me at the café about five if you want to."

Somewhere around ten-o-clock, Shorty was dosing when a loud banging rattled the door. "Alfonso! Open the door! Why you don't come for tequila tonight? Alfonso, are you in there?"

Shorty jerked his pistol and had it cocked as he slowly unlocked the door. It was dark, and the three Mexicans couldn't see Shorty as they walked in. "Why do you not have a lamp lit?"

"Because you'd see my gun stuck in yore fat belly! If any of you make a move for a gun this fat bastard gets two slugs to the gut! Tell um hombre!"

"Do as he says, he has a gun right in my belly."

"Alright, I want to hear three guns hitting the floor. If yer dumb enough to think you can get off a shot, go ahead and try. I'll gut shoot your friend then kill you both."

Guns dropped to the floor then Shorty reached into his left shirt pocket for a match. Handing it to the one with the gun in his belly, Shorty told him to light a lamp.

As light flooded the room, the men stood like small kids that had just been caught doing something wrong. "Why you do this *Señor?* We do nothing."

"Yeah I know and I'm gonna see you don't get the chance. Now walk toward then bars." Shorty reached for the cell key.

As he walked them inside, one of them said, *"Señor, do you not know if you do this thing you will be killed?"*

As he turned the key in the lock he said, "I'd say I'd have a hell of a lot better chance of being killed if I didn't lock y'all up. Now y'all had better get some sleep, yer gonna be here awhile."

"Only until tomorrow, *gringo!* Tomorrow you die!"

As Shorty dosed in a chair with his feet on the desk, he heard them talking for hours. J R was expecting up to three dozen Mexicans to be at his shop well before noon tomorrow. *'Stan has got to warn the town's people an get um somewhere safe.'*

Right at five-o-clock, Shorty got the key to the front door and started to walk out. One of the men hollered, "Hey *gringo,* we need something to eat and coffee."

"Alright, I'll see you get fed." He walked out and locked the door. He was the first at the café and had one cup of coffee in him by the time Stan walked in with Bud, David and Leo.

They all ordered coffee and breakfast. While waiting for their meal, Shorty talked asking Stan if he had anyone that could take food to the prisoners and stand by as guard.

Bud spoke up, "Shorty, I'll be glad to do it. I'll feed um then lock that door and sit there with loaded shotguns till you come an tell me its all clear."

"That sounds good, but if things start getting loud an rough at that front door, you get yore ass out back and beat it around to the livery. No need in getting all shot up."

Stan looked around saying, "Now Shorty, I talked to several people last night and we've got help, men that will use their guns."

"Alright but I want all of you to set up around the livery, and protect businesses on both sides of the street at the west end of town, along the river. I'll let the cavalry know where y'all will be. When shooting starts some of J R's men might try running back this'a way, headed for the crossing and Mexico."

He thought a minute, "Stan, it'd be best if you could get a couple of men to stay at the jail and help Bud. Him feeding them fellers alone could get rough."

Stan called the owner of the café over and filled him in on what was about to happen. "You wait right here. I will get my two sons to help with the jail. They will not be afraid to shoot. They will hold shotguns on the prisoners and if anyone tries to come through the front door, they will shoot them also."

"That sounds good to me. That jail being made out of adobe, they can hold off a small army. But I think all them other fellers will be too damn busy trying to save their own hides."

As they stood to leave, Bud and the two young men took coffee and food with them. Stan told Shorty he already had a horse saddled for him.

Fifteen minutes later Shorty was on his way to the fort. As he rode up to the gate, the men let him ride on in. Stopping in front of the General's office, he dismounted just as Sergeant Jenkins came walking up.

Paul L. Thompson

"Well Shorty, the General listened when I showed him Private Reynolds rifle. The private was the general's orderly and was well liked. The general now realizes none of the men deserted, that gun runner killed um."

"How many men are we taking from here?"

"I was just about to go in and ask the general that."

As they walked in, there stood the general in full battle gear, including his pistol around his waist. "Marshal, I was dead wrong. Everything you said was true. You have looked the situation over, what is your assessment of the area?"

"I think it'll be pretty easy on us being as that gun shop is only a block north of the river. I have already got a gob of town's people staked out on the west end of town, from the livery on west. If half your troops line up along the river and the other half ride right down the street, we'll have um surrounded. Now they are expecting two er three dozen Mexicans from Juarez to show up before noon. They were going to get your troops out of the fort on a wild goose chase and hit your armory again. Then they were riding down river and do the same at Fort Hancock."

"Good Lord! If they had gotten away with it, neither fort would have been able to defend its self from any raid. Marshal, how in the world did you happen upon this operation?"

"Well Sir, it all started over a new kind of rifle. Every outlaw that read about it has tried getting it. J R did, but I lucked out and got it back. Everything else was pure accidental. I was already thinking that rifle has caused a lot of trouble, now I see it's going to save a bunch of lives. Now how many men are you taking?"

"I am going to leave that up to you and Sergeant Jenkins. As many as you think we will need."

Shorty looked over at Jenkins. "What'da ya think, sixty er so? We may get into trouble if them Mexicans hear

176

the gunfire and come to help. They're wanting the rifles J R promised them."

Before Jenkins could answer the general did. "Then if that is the case, we will take a hundred troopers and leave twenty of them to guard the river crossing. Sergeant, inform the men and see they have a hundred rounds of ammunition for every rifle. We will ride within the hour."

Shorty looked at him, "Yer going too?"

"This battle I would not miss for the world. Any of those men that survive will face my firing squad. That is Americans and Mexicans alike. This will send a message to the Mexican rebels the United States will fight to protect its borders. After the fact, I will notify the Mexican Government. Perhaps they will round up the ones still in Mexico."

"I've took back the sheriff's office and have two gringos and five Mexicans locked up. I left three men guarding them."

"Then we will stop by and pick them up on our way back to the fort. Are you ready to ride?"

Thirty minutes later, on the west end of town they stopped and split forces. Twenty men dismounted and took up positions to cover the river crossing. Thirty men rode on down river, scattering out along the bank behind the gun shop. Sergeant Jenkins stayed with this bunch.

Shorty, the general and forty-five men slowly rode down the street. As they past the livery Shorty shouted, "It's about to start. David, you and Leo get in the hay loft where you can see farther down the street and warn anybody if they head this'a way."

Three blocks, then two, now one away from the gun shop. Not one man was seen. The general was getting worried. "Marshal, do you think they somehow got word and have gone?"

"Nope, I think most of um are in there dead assed

asleep with a hangover. They'll start stirring about after a bit. We just need to get your men under cover across the street and see what they try."

They waited almost an hour before men started walking out the back door, going to the outhouse. Sergeant Jenkins saw this and acted at once. "You, you and you come on! We're grabbing any man that comes out to take his morning dump."

Within a half hour they had six men, when one man in the shop got tired waiting his turn and stuck his head out the back door, just as two soldiers walked a man down the path toward the river. He jerked back inside and shouted, "J R! The cavalry just grabbed Sully and I don't see none of the others."

J R quickly gave orders as he glanced at the clock on the wall. "All we have to do is hold um, off another half hour and we'll have help from Mexico. Get yore rifles and get to windows covering the front and back. Shoot any bastard you see."

Sergeant Jenkins had just started back up the path when a bullet knocked him sideways and down in the tall brush. Ten guns opened fire and blew that window out, killing the shooter. Two men crawled off to one side of the trail and grabbed Jenkins under both arms, pulling him back to the river.

"Sarge, how bad is it?"

"You member that wasp that got me in the ear last year?"

"Yeah."

"Well that hurt worse. Did either of you get my rifle?"

"Yeah, its right here."

"Okay. I want you to circle around front to Shorty and the general. You tell um in ten minutes were gonna hit that back door with all we've got. Tell um not to shoot us as we run um out the front. Hurry, a minute of that ten is gone."

Shorty and the general had waited, wanting to see what that shooting was all about. A private came running around behind a store on the north side of the street just as the general was about to give the word to open fire.

"Hold it Sir! Hold it!"

"What's wrong Private?"

"In six minutes Sergeant Jenkins is going to mount a full attack on the back side of the building. There is only two windows and one door. He knows when they open up and keep firing with over thirty guns, those men will exit the building through the front, unless they know you are here waiting."

"Well said, Private. Hold your fire men, until you see men coming out that door. Give um plenty of room and maybe we'll get them all."

Four minutes later, bullets started slamming through the back windows and into the door. Boards split, windows had shattered and now the door was slowly falling apart from the shear number of bullets that ripped through it.

J R knew they were in trouble and could not hold out until the Mexicans arrived. He had several dead and dying men all over the store. "Come on! Out the front, we'll make it to the crossing and maybe the Mexicans will see we're in trouble and ride to help."

At that very moment, the soldiers watching the crossing opened fire on over three dozen Mexicans that were riding to help J R. They rode hard and fast, several were killed, but the others reached the dry bank and rode on north away from the gunfire. Circling back, they headed for the gun shop. They were going to get the rifles J R had stored, then cross the river miles down stream back to Mexico.

Just as J R and his men ran into the street and before Shorty and the general opened fire, here came two dozen Mexicans. "They made it! By damn they heard the gunfire and came to help." J R started waving to let them know who he was. A bullet took him smack dab in the face. His men started firing at the Mexicans just as General Jordan's men opened fire on all of them.

The Mexicans were riding at full speed and could not stop their horses in time. Men and horses were down with some of J R's men making it back to the porch and beside the building.

With cover their shots were more accurate. Mexicans were falling from their horses and cavalrymen were being slammed back dead. Several Mexicans got their horses turned and headed back for the crossing. That did no good as Stan, David and Leo with a dozen town's men were waiting. When the firing stopped, nine of J R's men and fourteen Mexican were alive, with most of them being wounded. The general had seven men dead and ten wounded with three of those very severe.

A bullet had bounced off the left side of Sergeant Jenkins head and knocked him goofy for a couple of minutes, but he is alright and helped round up the rest of J R's outlaws.

"Well Marshal, we did it. Now I have to send a trooper to the fort for my two doctors and wagons enough to take the wounded. I will have my men give the town folks a hand at cleaning up this mess." He looked around. "Sergeant Turner, secure that building until wagons arrive to remove all government property."

CHAPTER FIFTEEN

I t took two days cleaning up dead horses and men. J R's building was gone through and the rifles and ammunition removed and taken to the fort. The people of El Paso tried to get Stan to take the job of sheriff. He thanked them, but said he was not a law man. They needed someone with experience.

Shorty suggested a friend of his that was retired. "I'm sure Joe will give you a hand until he could train a law man. If you want I'll wire him at once."

One of the town fathers asked, "What's his name and where has he been sheriff?"

"Joe Buckles was the best sheriff Amarillo Texas ever had. He started out as a Texas Ranger."

"And yer sure you could get him to come down here?"

"Should, he owes me a few favors. Now he's a no nonsense sheriff. You break the law he will arrest you and throw you in jail. Then it will be up to a judge to what happens to you."

The mayor and town fathers mumbled among them selves then told Shorty to send for him. "Let him know we'll pay fifty dollars a month and stall and feed for his horse. Also all bullets and whatever else he needs pertaining to his office."

That evening Shorty rode to the fort on his borrowed horse. Sergeant Jenkins was glad he dropped by before leaving town. They walked inside to talk with the general. General Jordan stood and extended his hand. "Marshal, you know I can not thank you and the town of El Paso enough for what you did. I and the Mexican Government will be sending wires to the President letting him know how much we have gained by you being here. You helped save the town along with keeping me and this fort from looking like a bunch of asses. If you are ever back down this way, please stop in and say hello."

"I'll do that General. I'll be headed for Las Cruces in about an hour. The train ride don't take all that long, so I'll get a good night's sleep before going on to Chloride."

Three days later they arrived in Chloride and Shorty said he would be headed home in the morning. David said hello to his father and told what happened. "Pop, I'm gonna ride out and let Margret know I'm back."

"You do that son."

Thirty minutes later he rode past the fields and saw Mister Thomas and Chester Bain out hoeing weeds. He waved and rode on to the house. Margret was sitting in the porch swing and called out, "Hello David. When did you get back?"

"About an hour ago an came right out as soon as I could." A mischievous grin came to Margret's face.

"You really shouldn't have. I didn't know but what you had been killed or something awful like that had happened. I waited for days and hearing no word, I got married."

"You what? Got married! To who?"

"Chester Bain, he's out working with father now."

"Chester Bain!" It felt as thought a horse had kicked him in the chest with both back feet. "Oh no, oh no. Margret why didn't you wait? You must have knowed I love you with all my heart. I never even thought anything about you not waiting for me."

Margret was almost feeling bad at seeing how heart broken David was, but kept the farce going a bit longer. "If you really loved me, you would have told me and then I would have waited."

"But darn it Margret, I thought you knowed. Dear Lord, I thought you knowed." Tears filled his eyes.

Dejected, heart broken and with slumped shoulders, David slowly turned to walk away. "Just a moment, David," She got up, walked over and looked him in the eyes. "David Graham, I love you too." She threw her arms around his neck and kissed him full on the mouth. David melted into it then jerked back.

"What about Chester?"

"Silly, I would never marry anyone but you. I just said that to see what kind of reaction I would get."

"You bout broke my heart is what you went an done. Please don't ever tease me that'a way again."

"Okay I won't if you will marry me."

"Oh yes I'll marry you. I was going to ask on your birthday anyhow." He pulled her to him and held her in his arms, softly kissing her full lips. "When can we tell every body?"

"Right now, as soon as daddy gets that smile off his face."

"Huh?" David turned and there stood Mister Thomas. "Sir I… Well you know."

"Yeah I know, Margret all ready told me."

"Told you what?"

"That she was gonna marry you."

"Well she sure didn't get that wrong. I'll let Pop know as soon as I get back to town. Uh Margret, when are we gonna do this?"

"Anytime, I already have all my things packed and my wedding dress bought. How about this Sunday before church?"

"Alright, I think I can wait that long. I'll be out tomorrow." He got his horse and rode back to the store.

Bob was just closing and told him to go ahead and take care of his horse and he would meet him over at Kathy and Bill's café. Bob looked up and said, "You seem mighty happy about something. Glad to be back home?"

"Yeah Pa, I really am. See you at the café."

As they ate supper, David told his dad he and Margret were going to be married this coming Sunday. Bob hollered out, "Hey Bill! You an Kathy get out here! I have some important news.'

Bill and Kathy stepped from the kitchen, Bill drying his hands on a towel as Kathy wiped hers on her apron. "What's so important?" They saw the smile on Bob's face.

"David and Margret are gonna get married this Sunday."

Bill said really, and turned to Kathy, who just smiled and said, "That ain't news. I've knowed that for nigh on to a week."

"You did!"

"Sure, I went with Margret to pick out her wedding dress. Right pretty dress for a mighty pretty girl. David, you couldn't have done no better. She's a good'un."

David asked Shorty to stay for the wedding, but he said he had been away from the ranch too long now. He saddled up and rode off early the next morning. David and Margret both picked Leo as David's best man.

Sunday morning moments before the wedding, the stage rolled in with two men in business suits as the only passengers. They checked into the hotel and asked where they might find David Graham. The hotel manager looked at the clock and said, "Right about now he's standing in front of the preacher, getting married. Are you gentlemen friends of the family?"

"No, we have not had the pleasure of meeting him as of yet. We came all the way from Patterson, New Jersey to do just that."

"David Graham! You came all this way to see David!"

"Yes, why is that so surprising as he is a well known boy in the circle of firearms invention. Word does get about when someone comes up with a new rifle or any other kind of firearm."

"I suppose you could go to the wedding, though it has already started. Perhaps you could attend the reception. It will be at the town hall within the hour."

"In the mean time, where could we get a good meal?"

"Can't, Bill an Kathy are at the wedding. Oh wait, Salazar has a small café two blocks down the street and a half block south."

"Thank you, will you be at the reception?"

"Yes, if not having to wait on the stage, I'd been at the wedding myself. Those are two nice young people."

An hour later the town hall was full, as the two business men made their way around tables to find a standing place along the west wall. Young and old were dancing to a fiddle, two guitars and a mouth harp. The newly weds were easy to spot as David guided Margret around the floor.

After several minutes, Sheriff Dobbs eased over beside the two gentlemen. "Heard you fellows were here to see David Graham. That right?"

"Yes, yes it is, Sheriff." The men stuck out their hands to shake. "I am Jason Blake, and this is Mathew Coffer. We will not interrupt the celebration, but perhaps we will be able to talk with Mister Graham sometime in the morning."

Dobbs looked both men in the eyes. "Your business with David wouldn't happen to be about a rifle, would it?"

"Yes it is. We got word there was a new kind of gun in the small town of Chloride, New Mexico Territory and were sent here to look it over."

"Then you mean David no harm?"

"Harm! My goodness no! We are business men looking for new firearms."

"Alright, I'll let David know you'll be in to see him at, oh say nine-o-clock in the morning at the grocery and mercantile store. So you will know I will also be there. The store is up the street a half block from the hotel."

"Thank you Sheriff, nine-o clock is fine with us."

The reception started breaking up around four, as farmers and ranchers had to get on home and take care of their livestock and do chores. Women also had supper to fix for their families. Kathy and Bill had already invited Margret and David to eat supper at the café. Kathy had a surprise planned.

At six-o-clock, the café was full of people as David and Margret walked in. Tables were together and right in the middle was a white wedding cake. On top, written with chocolate icing were their names and two small hearts. Margret grabbed Kathy and gave her a big hug.

"Oh Kathy, thank you so much. I know that is what my mother would have done."

As every one ate supper and plenty of cake, the two business gentlemen walked in and got a corner table. Kathy served them supper then asked if they would like a piece of wedding cake.

"If it would not be too much trouble, thank you."

The men never noticed Sheriff Dobbs keeping a close eye on them. He was making sure nothing went wrong on this wedding day. This was a happy time for the whole town.

At ten minutes before nine, Sheriff Dobbs walked into the store. David was stacking cartridges on the shelf behind the counter. "Good morning Sheriff. Something I can get you?"

"Naw, but yer gonna have a couple of visitors here in a few minutes. You'd better strap on that rifle and be ready just in case."

David never hesitated, just quickly strapped on the holster then checked the rifle as he clipped it to his leg. "Think it could be trouble?"

"No idea, hope not."

At nine-o-clock sharp, the two men walked in. Bob and David were behind the counter, with Sheriff Dobbs kind'a over to one side with the thong off the hammer of his pistol.

The men walked right to the counter and extended their hands for a shake. They introduced them selves then said they were here to see a new gun. "We got word about your rifle as well as your exploits using it, and were sent here to take a look for ourselves. May we look your rifle over?"

David looked from them to Dobbs then his father. Dobbs put his hand on the butt of his pistol and nodded, while Bob stepped to his right and put his hand on a gun he had under the counter.

David slowly removed the rifle and holster then unloaded the rifle before handing it across the counter. Both men quickly examined it from barrel to stock and could not believe their eyes. Placing the rifle back on the counter, they went over the holster like they were handling a new born baby.

With smiles on their faces, one of them asked, "Will you be acquiring a Patent on both the rifle and holster?"

David glanced at his father then over at Sheriff Dobbs. "No, I can't do that."

"Can't! Why not? This is the most fantastic rifle since the repeater came out in the 60's. It will revolutionize the swiftness one can fire a rifle. One man could do the same as several. Every lawman in America would want one."

"Well Sir, I didn't make this rifle. A friend of mine did."

"You didn't! Is he where we may speak with him? We have crossed this nation just to look at this rifle."

"Yeah, I suppose I could take you over to talk with him. Sheriff, you want to come along?"

"Wouldn't think of doing anything else."

They walked out and down the street to the livery. One of the men said, "We do not ride horses. We will rent a buggy."

"Naw, no need in that, he owns the livery."

There was a sigh of relief as they walked in and David

called out for Leo. Leo walked from a stall and said, "Yeah, what'da ya need?" He was looking at the two men in business suits.

"A couple of fellows here that want to meet you."

Leo stepped forward with his hand out. "Leo Patterson."

"What a coincident, we work for the Patterson Firearms Company and both owners are also Leo Patterson."

"Yeah, that'd be my father and grandfather."

"Father, grandfather!" Both men seemed in shock.

"Yes Sir, I am Leo Patterson the fifth."

"Good Lord Boy! Why haven't you gone home and patented that rifle? Your father and grandfather sent us all this way to acquire the manufacturing rights."

Leo looked at them for almost a full minute then glanced over at David. "Give me a couple of days and I'll give you my answer. I have to talk a few things over with David."

"Then you will consider going back to Patterson with us?"

"No I will not! At least not to stay. This is my home and will not leave as long as the mines hold out. All of my friends are here. I will only consider giving father the rights to manufacture the rifle. Now if you gentlemen will excuse me, I have work to do."

Everyone left except David. As Leo grabbed the wheelbarrow to start cleaning stalls, David picked up a shovel and gave him a hand. "What'er you thinking, Leo?"

He let go of the wheelbarrow handles with a smile on his face. "How would you like to be rich? I mean really rich."

"But Leo, I am rich! I have Margret, dad and you as the best fishing an hunting friend anybody could ever have. Dad and I make a good living, so what else do I need."

"Yeah but David, these mines are already slowing down. A year, two at the most and they will close. Then this town will die as all other boom towns have done. Without the mines, there is no way for people to make a living."

"Now that's something to think about. We wouldn't even be able to sell the store. We would just have to pack up, walk off and leave it. We'd just have to find another town and start over."

"Yeah but if we patented that…"

"We! What do you mean, we?"

"It's your rifle David. If you knew how to use a pistol to start with, I'd never thought of making that rifle for you. It's darn sure more yours than mine."

David sat down on a bale of hay, rolling everything over in his mind. "Leo, you have more schooling than I do. I'll go along with anything you think is right. No matter, we stay friends."

"You have that right, friends are more important than money any day. When I got to this town, if I hadn't met you and your father I probably wouldn't have stayed. You remember that first day I walked into y'alls store an we got to talking. Within an hour you had me down at the creek fishing."

"Yeah, that was fun, huh?"

"Yeah. Okay here's what I'm thinking, see if you agree. I'll take the rifle and holster and go back to Patterson with these fellers and get a patent in both our names. I'll sign a manufacturing contract with Patterson Firearms Company getting ten thousand dollars up front. Then we will get a royalty on every rifle and holster sold from now on."

"Lord! Do you really think they'd go along with that?"

"I don't see why not. It's a new gun that nobody can make unless we give them a contract. They want it bad, or they wouldn't have sent two men all this way. To cinch the deal, I might even mention Winchester er Colt."

"You'd let Winchester er Colt make um!"

"Heck no, but dad and grandpa don't know that."

David stood and stuck out his hand. "Alright, you have your self a partner. Is it alright if I tell Margret and dad?"

"Sure, they'll need to know you are going to be very rich."

Before Leo left to go with the men to New Jersey, he got Bud to run the livery. David and Margret went to see him off. Standing on the walkway while luggage was loaded up top the stage and being tied down, Leo reached in his pocket and handed David a thousand dollars.

"What's this for?"

"I want you and Margret to go up to Denver, Colorado and look the town over. Matter of fact why don't you look the whole country over? That is one town that will not die when mining dies out. There is mining all through those mountains and ranches and farms for sixty miles or more."

"Why Denver?"

"Because I think it would be a good place to live and raise a family. You can buy your father another business up there and stop worrying about these mines around here closing. Remember David, in no time you will have more money than you've ever seen in your whole life."

"Alright we'll do it. I'll talk with dad and see what he says. We'll be back way before you are."

"Yeah, but take your time and really look things over."

They all waved as the stage left Chloride, headed for the railroad where Leo and the two men would board the train to New Jersey. Margret took David's arm and leaned against him. "Why would Leo do all of this for us?"

"Because we are very good friends, as close as any brothers could ever be. I wish everyone could have a friend as good as Leo. Now come on, let's go talk to Pop about us going to Denver."

Bob was excited, and told them so. "Now David, if you do find Denver is where you would like to live, you must know I'll be staying here for awhile."

"Why, we will buy you another business up there, even better than this one."

"That is no problem, as I have more than enough money to relocate. I just can not leave this town and my friends that need and depend on this store. When and if the mines close, then you'll see me in Denver. It would also be best if y'all went out and talked with Seth. He surly will miss his only daughter."

"Oh we will, but you know we will only be gone a couple of weeks this first trip. Who knows, by the time we get back you might have changed your mind about going."

"I doubt that, we'll see. I'll even talk with Seth."

It took a few days planning and packing for the trip, but at last they were on their way. Neither had ever been to Denver and were looking forward to the trip and being away from Chloride.

On this very day, Dick and Nell had gone in and talked with Curly. Telling him they needed to go into Rifle and catch the train to Denver. Dick told Curly he had to go and take care of some business for his mother. Really, he wanted to go open a bank account for all the money he and Albert had in their saddlebags. Several times they had been worried some of the hands would stumble upon it. He could not put it in the bank in Rifle, how would he ever explain how he got his hands on that much money?

More than once he and Albert had gotten together trying to figure out how much money they took from each bank so they could send it back, as they did for the bank of Alma. After months, they made up their minds just to keep it and somehow do only good with it, never spending another dime of it on them selves. After all this time, they seldom ever thought of Edgar and Jeff. Only that they were free of those brothers and happily so.

On Tuesday morning Dick and Nell arrived in Denver. This was the first time either had been in such a large town.

After getting a hotel room and eating dinner, they went looking for a bank. The Colorado Ranchers Bank caught Dick's eye.

"Let's try here."

They walked in and asked the teller if they could open an account. "Yes most certainly. Mister Shoemaker will assist you. That is his desk right over there." He pointed to a desk with a nice looking gentleman talking with another customer. They sat and waited.

When finished with that customer, Mister Shoemaker stood and walked over to the chairs where Dick and Nell were sitting. "Were you waiting to see me?"

"Oh yes Sir. We would like to open an account."

"Right this way, please."

They walked over and took a chair as Shoemaker walked behind the desk. "And how much money would you be placing in the account, to start with?"

"Thirty-six thousand dollars."

"Thirty-six thousand!"

"Yes Sir, is there a problem?"

"No, not at all. I assume you can write."

"Oh yes Sir, my wife and I both write."

"Wonderful just fill out this form stating your name and mailing address. Will it be a joint account?"

"What's that?"

"Will you and your wife both be using the account?"

"Oh yes, but any deposits we make from now on will be done by mail."

"If I may ask, why is that?"

"We live on a ranch north and east of Rifle."

"That will be no problem. Just make sure you put your account number on any correspondence."

"What in the world is that? Correspondence."

Shoemaker smiled, "Write your account number on a piece of paper and send it along with any money you send.

That way it all goes into the proper account."

"Oh I see." Dick placed his saddlebags on the desk and got out the money, keeping six hundred dollars and putting that in his pocket. He counted out Thirty-six thousand and fifty nine dollars. "We will put all of this in your bank."

Mister Shoemaker recounted it and wrote that amount down on two pieces of paper. Handing one to Dick, "That is your receipt and the account number is at the top. Try not to lose that.

"Your receipt will always show your balance. Every time you spend or send money, we will send you a statement letting you know your current balance."

"Well we won't be spending all that much, but thank you." They stood and shook hands. Mister Shoemaker smiled at these young people, with a very bright future.

Dick felt better, as they walked out on the street. "Let's get something to eat then see every sight in town."

Nell had hold of his arm. "Good Lord, I've never seen so many people in my life. How do they all make a living, with no way to grow crops or raise cattle?"

"I'd say off of each other. One man works, gets paid and spends his money at some store that pays wages to some helper. Then that man buys groceries or whatever and so on. The money kind'a goes around in a circle."

Nell was looking around and said, "I'm just thankful we live on a ranch and work for Mister Goss. I'd feel all uncomfortable being around all these people. I like nice and quiet, this is not."

"Yeah me too, but we'll stay a couple of days and see the town. Just look at these brick streets. Now ain't that something, no mud to worry about."

They ate then walked around until almost sundown. "We'd better get on back to the hotel." As they walked along, two men stepped from an alley. Both had knives and demanded their money. Dick was taken back for just a moment but blurted out, "Mister, yer about to get shot dead!"

In the blink of an eye his forty-five was in his hand, cocked. "Now just you fellers hold on to them knives right tight like and walk out yonder in the middle of the street."

They started to put their hands up, but he told them no, just walk. In the middle of the street, he made them stop and stand still. By this time by-standers had already called for the police and word was past down.

A few minutes later, two uniformed officers came running up. They looked at Dick and Nell, with Dick holding a cocked pistol in his hand. One quickly dropped his hand to his sidearm, starting to draw it. Dick smiled, "I hope yer gonna use that on these two would be robbers. Look what they have in their hands."

The officers both looked and then smiled, "Willie and Wilford Dokes! Damn if it don't look like you jumped the wrong people this time. Drop them knives."

The men were quickly handcuffed and one officer turned to Dick and Nell. "Quick thinking young fellow, and yer lucky you wear a gun. We've been after these hombres for six months. Now there is a hundred dollar reward on these two, it's yours."

"Thank you Sir, but do you know somebody in real bad need that could use it?"

"Sure, but don't you want it?"

"No Sir, I'd rather it helped somebody that's hungry er something like that."

"Well I never heard..." He stuck out his hand for a shake. "Young fellow, there is a Mrs. Garrison over on Jackson Street that feeds homeless kids. This will be a blessing to her. Thank you."

"Yes Sir." He and Nell walked on to the hotel. As they walked into their room, Nell grabbed and kissed him.

"Oh Dick I love you so! That was the kindest thing I

have ever seen anyone do. Just the thought of you helping hungry children, will be in my heart forever."

For two days they walked the streets of Denver over, looking at tall buildings and the hundreds of people. They even bought a few things Nell thought she could use at the ranch. Out on the sidewalk they stopped and looked up at a seven story building with Nell saying she could not understand how men got all the way up there to build anything that high. "It looks like they would fall."

Dick laughed, "Well I wouldn't do it. Crawling on a bucking bronc is about as high as I want to get. We'd better get on to the hotel and get everything packed up. We'll be leaving on the six-o-clock morning train."

"Okay, but let's just eat in the hotel café tonight. I'm a bit too tired to go walking anymore today."

"Yeah I guess we've walked more in the past couple of days than in the last year. Oh, before we leave we want to get Curly a new pair of boots. He's patched them of his just about all he can."

"Oh yes, he'll like that."

CHAPTER SIXTEEN

D avid and Margret stepped down from the train and looked at all the people rushing around, as they waited for their luggage. A young fellow about David's age asked, "Would you like your luggage delivered to the hotel?"

David looked at him then over at Margret. "Naw, I'll take it. It ain't all that much." He reached in his pocket and handed the fellow a dime.

"Thank you Sir, have a nice stay in Denver."

After being told the hotel was a block and a half up the street, they headed that way just as a man climbed a ladder and started lighting street lamps. Margret stopped and watched. "Will you look at that? They have lamps right on the street!"

They got to the hotel and checked in. The hotel in Chloride was nothing like this. Margret just couldn't quit looking all around. "Sir, your key. Your room is up those stairs and down the hallway, number two-twenty-four. Shall I have the boy take your luggage?"

"No thank you, but is that food I smell?"

"Yes it is our restaurant is one of the finest in Denver. It is just through that doorway. Will you be dressing for dinner?"

David looked at himself and at Margret. "We are dressed, what'd you think? We was gonna go in there naked?"

"Sir I… No Sir."

They went to the room and left the luggage. Margret walked over to a mirror to brush her hair. David walked around the room and looked through an open door.

"Margret! Look at this, it's one of them water toilets right in our room. Yeah and a big ol' bath tub big as a horse trough over against one wall."

"Naw!" She looked and smiled, "Good, I was about to ask where the outhouse was." She walked in and closed the door.

A few minutes later she walked out with a smile on her face. "I think I am going to like Denver. That place doesn't even stink."

"Ready?"

They walked down stairs and turned to their left, going through the double doors into a beautiful restaurant. Waiters in black pants and white shirts scurried from table to table, some carrying huge platters of food. A slender, elderly gentleman smiled and stepped forward, "Two for dinner?"

"Yeah there's two of us alright, but we came to eat supper. We had dinner on the train."

The man cracked another smile, "Right this way, please." He seated them at a table and said, "Your waiter will be right with you."

A young boy came rushing over and poured crystal goblets full of ice water, turned and quickly walked away. Margret looked after him, "Now how in the world did he know I'm thirsty?"

The waiter came and took their order then the water boy brought them ice tea. David was looking toward the back of the room and didn't see Dick and Nell as they started out of the restaurant, going to their room. Dick just happened to glance back to his left and almost stumbled into Nell.

"Honey, would you mind going on to the room alone? I think I would like to go in the bar and have a beer."

"Yes, I was going to ask if you could find something to do for awhile. I want to go up and take a long hot bath." He stood there and watched as Margret took the stairs and disappeared down the hallway. Gathering courage, he turned and quickly walked back into the restaurant.

Going straight to David and Margret's table, he pulled out a chair and sat down with out being asked. David and Margret turned at the sound of the chair, and with mouths open David started to stand. "Sit down. This won't take a minute."

Margret was a bit scared, but David was getting mad. Right now he wished he had his rifle. Dick said, "I mean you no harm. Ma'am, I'm just glad to see you are alive. Now before you go to screaming er hollering out, I have a gun and noticed you don't, so just be quiet for a minute.

"First off me nor my brother shot nobody, not you nor that teller, not nobody else. I worried something awful when Edgar shot you. After that second robbery, which we knew nothing about at the time, me an my brother rode off and ain't looked back.

"Jeff and Edgar was the ones that shot you and the teller and robbed the bank the second time. I don't know how much money they got, but the first robbery was for three hundred and sixteen dollars. Are y'all going back to Chloride?"

"Yes but, why do you want to know?"

"I'm giving you four hundred dollars to give that bank. If I knew how much Jeff an Edgar got, I'd pay that back too."

"That money was recovered and a lot more when those two were killed over in Socorro. Why are you doing this?"

"Trying to make amends for some wrong me an my brother went an done. I am married now and living a clean new life. Just seeing you alive, means I won't have to live with your death on my mind for the rest of my life. It also gave me the courage to come let you know I didn't shoot you."

"I know you didn't, I saw the boy very clearly that did."

"I know it'll be hard, but I hope one day you and that

town can forgive us for what we done. Did the teller have a family?"

"No, if he did no one knew of it, maybe back east."

Dick stood and handed David four hundred dollars. "That's for the bank. Again, please try to forgive me and I wish you both well." He turned to walk out but David stopped him.

"Can you stay a minute longer? We won't call out or anything like that."

Dick turned back to the table. Margret said, "Please sit back down, for just a moment." Dick dropped into the chair.

David said, "I'm sure you have heard everything happens for a reason. You know, good or bad."

"Yes, I've heard that saying and wondered on it somewhat."

"Well it's like this, after your friend shot Margret, I went to a friend of mine and he made me a new gun to protect myself with. He is now in New Jersey getting a patent on the gun and holster and we will be very rich. That is what we are doing in Denver, looking the town over so we can move up here. If shooting Margret hadn't happened, there would be no new gun, we would not be rich and we would be in Chloride until the mines shut down."

A small smile came to Dick's lips. "Yes and if Jeff and Edgar hadn't robbed that bank one more time, I would not have left New Mexico Territory and would have never met my wife. Then just maybe in time you can forgive us after all."

As Dick stood, so did David and stuck his hand out for a shake. "And Margret and I wish you and your wife well." Dick walked out, feeling much better and went to the bar for a beer.

The next morning at six, Dick and Nell were on the train headed up the mountain to Rifle. David and Margret were eating breakfast, getting ready to look Denver over.

Nell snuggled against Dick saying, "I think you enjoyed getting away from the ranch and seeing a big town."

"Yes I did and feel better than I have in months. I can hardly wait till we get back so I can tell Albert all about it."

She looked up at him smiling, "Do you think Albert and Rachel will get married? They'd make a cute couple."

"Might, they seem hooked on one another."

"Do you think we'll ever get to come back to Denver?"

"Without a doubt, we'll do it once a year. I'd even like to find out more about that Mrs. Garrison and the homeless boys she feeds. That might be very interesting." He was thinking of thirty six thousand dollars just setting in that bank.

Over the next two weeks, David and Margret had seen every inch of Denver and the country close by. They saw beautiful neighborhoods with children playing in yards that looked like green pastures. Prosperous businesses lined every street down town and on roads leading into the country.

They talked to bankers and businessmen from one end of town to the other. There was nothing about this town they didn't like. As they ate supper on the last night they were to be in town, a boy came into the hotel restaurant calling out for a Mister David Graham.

David stood up where the boy could see him. "I'm David Graham."

"A telegram Sir." He handed David the telegram and asked him to sign a piece of paper he held in his hand.

"What's that for?"

"So the telegraph office will know I delivered the message, and didn't just throw it away."

"Thank you." David gave him a dime and the boy smiled.

Reading the telegram, David smiled and said, "It's

from Leo. He says the deal is done and they will start making rifles right away. He is on his way back to Chloride with ten thousand dollars, and his father is with him. It seems his father wants to meet the town's people that are such good friends of his son.

The next morning they were on their way home. David could hardly wait to get back so he can tell his father all about Denver. Margret leaned into his shoulder, "Oh David, I hope we do make lots of money. That way we can bring father up here to live with us. That dry land farm will be his early death."

Three days later David and Margret were back in Chloride and Leo should arrive any day. Monday morning all the miners were laid off at the Dillard mine. Silver ore had played out to where it was no longer profitable to stay in operation.

They were moving their operation over the mountains to Mogollon. Any miner could show up there and still have a job. Mister Dillard went around Chloride, paying all the mines bills and thanked the merchants for the credit. Dillard was one of Bob's biggest customers.

"Don't worry David we still have enough business to get by. There are still four working mines in the area. Though we will lose fourteen working families, we will make out."

Two days later Leo and his father came in on the stage. David was there to meet him and was introduced to Leo's father. They walked to the livery where Bud reached for a hand shake saying he needed to get home for a few hours. "Go ahead, and thanks for your help. When you get back I'll pay what I owe you." Leo smiled and opened a large almost flat box.

"Dad, help me hold this up. What do you think of this, David? This is called advertizing."

It was a beautiful poster in full color that read: A New

Gun. The easiest shooting, fastest firing rifle-pistol on the market today. One new gun takes the place of both a rifle and pistol. Join thousands of lawmen and order yours today. The Patterson Firearms Company, Patterson New Jersey. The pictures looked just like the real thing. Rifle and holster was displayed for all to see. These would be plastered all over every gun shop in America.

"Wow, you sure did something pretty alright. I'll bet y'all are tired. Why don't you take your father on over to the hotel and I'll watch the livery for awhile."

"Are you sure, I might be gone awhile."

"Yeah go ahead, I'll close at sundown and pick up Margret and Dad and we'll meet you at the café around seven."

On the way to the hotel, at seeing Leo was back, people hollered howdy and yelled how good it was to see him. Walking into the hotel, Mister Mason smiled right big, "Leo my boy, I sure have missed you around here. Its dad gummed sure good to see you back. We've all missed you"

"Howdy Mister Mason, this is my father, Leo Patterson."

"Mister Patterson, it is a pleasure Sir. And will you be staying with us long?"

"A few days, more or less."

"Sign right here and your room is number nine, right down that hallway."

Leo helped his father with his luggage and asked if he was tired and wanted to rest up awhile before supper. "No not at all, I want to go out and see this town you have called home for so long. It took us most forever getting here."

"You'll like these friendly folks Father, and just wait until you meet Kathy and Bill and taste their food. You will want to stay."

Everywhere they went it was the same, every person was sincerely happy to see Leo. Miners waved and hollered

David Graham, The New Gun

as they made their way to the saloon for a few beers before heading home to supper.

Just before seven they walked into the café, where Leo introduced his father to Kathy and Bill. "Mister Patterson, I suppose you all ready know, but this town is quite proud of your son."

Mister Patterson wasn't smiling when he asked, "And why would that be? Why would you or any of these people be proud of Leo? What is so special about him?"

You could have heard a pen drop. Kathy walked right up to the table. "Sir, he is a very nice boy and a hard worker. When he came to our town, the hostler at the livery was a drunk and never got anything done. Leo bought that place and cleaned it up and runs it as well as any man could.

"And while I'm at it I'll tell you something else. We use to have animals all about with bad feet because of the way they were shod. That is not the case anymore and he doctors' animals better than any doctor doctors' people. Yes Sir, we are proud. Now what do y'all want for supper?" Kathy wasn't sure if he was just a smart ass or thought no one could or should be proud of his boy.

Kathy and Bill brought out pot roast and biscuits with plenty of coffee and ice tea. Margret and the women mumbled among them selves while the men talked. Seth had come in from the farm and joined in welcoming Leo back.

The table was cleaned of everything but tea glasses and coffee cups which had been refilled. Seth looked over and said, "Well Leo, Margret and David sure did like Denver and one of these days me an Bob just might move up there too."

"Yes I really like that town. I came through there before making my way here to Chloride. In my mind I figured one day I'd go back there maybe to live."

Mister Patterson almost scoffed, "Then Son, how in the world would you wind up in a dusty spot on the side of a mountain in the middle of nowwhere, instead of a bustling city?"

"The people, Father. It was an easy choice because these are truly kind, gentle caring people. They became my friends at once and we all help one another in our daily lives."

Bob looked at Mister Patterson but spoke to David, Margret and Leo. "Well you young folks have a life of yore own to live, but as long as this town last, we'll stay and you will be missed."

Mister Patterson asked, "I really think it is only because of all his money is why he is liked so well?"

Seth looked over at him, "What money?"

"Leo's money, are you going to sit there and try to tell me you have no idea who this boy is? I and his family are among the top ten wealthiest families in America"

Seth let his eyes close to a slit, as Leo stood up, turned and stomped out of the café, with David following. "Well whoop tee doo! Who gives a big fat hogs butt! Mister, this town will miss the best hostler we ever had and nobody, I mean nobody ever knowed he had more than a few dollars to his name. He is a friend, a damn good friend an nobody gives a damn if he's flat assed broke or the Queen of France. Mister you might not know it, but all the damn money in the world can't buy true friends." He stood up, eyes flashing anger. "Goodnight!" If not for Leo, that Leo setting there would have some teeth missing.

Bob looked over at Margret as she sat there all wide eyed. He turned to Leo, "Mister Patterson, it seems as you have a pretty low opinion of the people of this town. If you…"

"Mister Graham, don't you go and think for one minute that I don't know Leo was coerced into signing away half of his patent to your son? Why he did it I have no idea. He and he alone made that rifle and it is rightfully every bit his and should only belong to the Patterson family. My soul purpose of coming to this God forsaken country was to offer your son enough money to get his name off that patent and contract. I am sure he can be bought off."

Margret pushed back the chair and quickly stood. "Mister, what kind of people do you think we are? You, you... Well you are!" She walked out with Bob following.

Kathy and Bill had heard every word, and as Mister Patterson sat drinking his tea, she walked to the table. She was mad, but held her temper as she said, "Mister Patterson, you are wrong about Leo, wrong about David and damn sure wrong about this town. I would thank you not to come into my café again and I hope your stay in Chloride is very short!"

He smiled, stood and dropped a twenty dollar gold piece on the table. Kathy quickly grabbed it and shoved it back into his open hand. "Keep it! I don't want your money. Now get!"

Leo and David had gone to the livery to talk. Bob and Margret went on home, very upset. Sitting on bales of hay, Leo had his face in his hands. "David, I should have known! Darn it all to heck I just should have known. Greed, money is the only reason he came here. I thought he was happy for me, proud of what I had accomplished on my own and wanted to meet the people that are my true friends. I so wanted that to be the case.

"If not for that rifle, he wouldn't have cared if he ever heard of me again. I so wanted...Oh how I wish there was someway out of that contract, but I know there isn't. Company lawyers draw those up where only the company can back out, if need be."

"But the contract is still good, ain't it? I mean they'll go ahead and make the rifle and holster an sell um."

"Oh yeah, they'll make million off of it wishing you and I were dead where the company would get it all."

"But if something happened to me, wouldn't Margret and Pop get my part?"

"Yes, if father's smart lawyers didn't screw them out of it. When we get to Denver, I will hire the best lawyer in Colorado and draw up a few new contracts between you and me. Then I will see a copy of each is delivered to the Patterson Firearms Company. I will also send my grandfather a telegram. Perhaps he knows nothing of what father is doing. He never seemed all greedy to me. He even talked with me, like he was interested in how I was."

"How long do you think your father will stay around here?"

"Oh he'll leave tomorrow as soon as we have our talk. If he thinks for one minute... Well never mind. You go on home to Margret. I'll just sit here a bit longer."

"Leo no matter what, you know you have me an Margret and this whole town."

"I know that David, thanks."

David walked in the house and asked his father where Margret was. "She's in y'alls bedroom. Son, she's mighty upset about what Leo's daddy went an said."

"Yeah, so is Leo. Bout broke his heart is what it done. He sure wanted his father to accept these town people as his friends."

He walked into the bedroom where Margret lay on the bed, eyes closed. She heard David and sit up. "Oh David, you and Leo didn't hear what that horrible man said about us and this town. Why can't he just love Leo for what he is and as we all do?"

"Leo said it was greed, he wants all of the money."

"What in the world will Leo do? I just know his heart has to be broken. I know your father nor mine would ever act that way."

"Leo is going to have a talk with his father. I think he will send him away. I know he is so ashamed for what his father put us all through, but it isn't his fault."

Leo slept in the hay loft and was at Kathy's front door as she opened at five-o-clock. "Come on in Leo, ready for that coffee?"

"Yes Ma'am, I sure need it this morning."

No one else was in the café this early, so Kathy poured herself a cup of coffee and sat at the table with Leo. She looked over at him, knowing he didn't know what to say. "Leo, none of us want you to think we don't understand. So your father don't like us, that's tough horse hockey. We don't much like him either, but we darn sure like you and will pay him no mind. You are one of us, a big part of our family. He will be gone before long and we will still be here together, all of us. Nothing as changed, except you got your feeling hurt."

He reached over and patted her on the hand. "Kathy, you and Bill have been more mother and father to me than my very own. Even my mother wouldn't have made me chicken soup when I came down sick. You did and brought it to me. She would have had the cook do it and the maid bring it up to my room.

"If she had time, she might have dropped by to tell me how horrible I sounded and looked. You are right Kathy, you, Bill and the people of this town are my family. Now, how about some biscuits and gravy before I starve to death"?

"Coming right up." She reached and squeezed his hand.

Just as he started eating, miners and town people started coming in. All said hello and went on with eating breakfast. None of them had heard what his father had said, or thought of this town. They were just glad he was back.

CHAPTER SEVENTEEN

"Son, why can you not understand that patent is rightfully yours? I will offer that boy ten thousand dollars and if he won't take that I'll make it twenty thousand. That patent must remain only in the Patterson family."

"No Father, you will do no such thing! Without David, Margret and this town there would be no new rifle. Why must you be so greedy?"

"Greedy! Son I am not greedy, I just want what is mine... Well yours. I will make that offer, and you will see how quickly he takes the money. That is all he is after then you can come on back home to New Jersey where you belong."

"Father you will not offer him anything! Why must you embarrass me in front of my friends?"

"These are not your friends! They are using you to get at my money! My money do you hear?"

"No Father, you will be on the ten-o-clock stage out of this town. I am staying and David, Margret and I are moving to Denver."

"I will not leave this town until I have that patent in my name! That is what I came for and will get no matter the cost!"

Leo stood, "Want'a bet!" He turned and walked out of the hotel and straight to the Sheriff's office.

At ten-o-clock, Sheriff Dobbs helped Mister Patterson aboard the stage. "Have a nice trip and don't come back to my town."

"I think it is a terrible day when the law sides with a town full of con-men and thieves against an honest business man. Helping them steal what is rightfully mine."

"Yeah, tell it your lawyers when you get back to New Jersey."

David stood beside Leo as they watched the stage disappear around the bend in the road. "What are we going to do now, Leo?"

"Get our things packed and be in Denver in front of a lawyer before he gets back home and tries cooking up something else. I'll give my livery to Bud and his family. I think he will make a good holster. Think you and Margret can be ready to pull out in a couple of days?"

"I don't see why not." They walked back to the livery then David went on to the store to talk with his father and Margret.

Six days later, David and Leo were in the law offices of Catron & Thompson. After Jim heard what was going on with a new rifle Leo had invented, James Catron smiled and said, "You came to the right place. Sherry is the best on things like this."

Sherry wanted to read the contract they had with the Patterson Firearms Company.

In just a few minutes she looked up and said, "This is an illegal contract and will not hold up in a court of law."

Leo looked at her, then over at David. "Illegal! How can that be? My father's lawyers drew it up. What are you saying?"

"Did you bring the contract back to Chloride where David could sign it? No you didn't as I see someone initialed it where David was supposed to sign. I am guessing by one of your father's lawyers. It is *'void ab inito'*."

"What in the world is ad abinito, or whatever you said?"

"Void, a nothing from the very beginning. This contract is unenforceable and I would say your father, as well as his lawyers know exactly that."

"What can we do?"

"I will send them papers telling them they have no contract, and why. If they continue manufacturing the rifle and holster, they will be sued. They will also return the rifle and holster you left with them to the rightful owner, one David Graham. Both you and David will sign the letter, as will I. They will have both of your addresses where they can ship the rifle and holster."

"Do you think they will?"

"They will or the whole bunch could wind up in prison and I'm sure they know that. We will not just sue I will prosecute if they do not follow the letter of the law."

Leo and David felt much better after talking with James and Sherry. As they walked back to the hotel Leo said, "Boy howdy that little red head sure sounded like she knew what she was doing."

"Yeah, but being as nobody will be making the rifle, what are we going to do for money?"

"Well we still have the ten thousand dollars, and I had several thousand I've saved up. I'll find me a little blacksmith shop and we'll make them ourselves. Now we won't make nigh the money as we could if they were being manufactured from scratch. I will have to buy the rifles and cut them down before we can sell them. Our profit won't be more than ten dollars per rifle, oh and maybe another five er six on the holster.

"When we save up enough money where I can buy the machinery, then we will start a full manufacturing plant."

"How long do you think that will take?"

"No more than a year at the most. But don't worry, with us both working we'll make out."

Over the next few days they found and bought a small two bedroom house and moved in. As David and Margret rearranged everything and hung curtains, Leo went back to visit Sherry.

He walked into the office and Jim looked up and said,

"Partner, you are one hard hombre to find."

"Yeah why's that?"

"I went to the hotel looking for you but they said you moved out leaving no forwarding address."

"Oh yeah, we bought a house over on Maple Street and have been buying furniture and moving in. Why were you looking for us? Something good I hope."

"Yep Sherry was right, as usual, and the contract is voided. They are mailing a voided copy to this office. It looks as if your father hires lawyers not quite as dumb as I was thinking."

"What about the rifle and holster?"

"That's what I wanted to talk with you about. They are not shipping it. Two men are bringing it along with a new contract for you and David both to sign."

"Well I'm here to tell you that is not going to happen! Deal with a crooked out fit and it's no telling where you'll get bit."

"Oh I most forgot, one of the men is your grandfather."

"Well at least it isn't father. Thanks Jim, for you and Sherry's help. Where's Sherry today?"

"In court. She's getting a fellow back his ranch that a couple of shyster bankers tried to steal."

"That wouldn't be the Colorado Ranchers Bank, would it?" That is where Leo and David had all their money and had just bought a house from them."

"Naw, it's the Collins Brother's Bank. The Colorado Ranchers Bank is a good honest, solid bank. It's our bank, no crooks there."

Two days later Leo had himself a small shop and had already bought ten rifles to start to work on. David was a quick learner and Leo showed him where and how to cut off the stock of the rifles and refinish them.

Margret was planting flowers and would make a small garden spot on the back side of the property. She was home alone when two men walked up the short walkway to the porch. She had just hung a basket of flowers and asked, "Yes, may I help you?"

"Yes Ma'am, I am Leo Patterson, Leo's grandfather and we would like to speak with him."

"He isn't here right now. They are down at the shop."

"Can you tell us where that is?"

"Yes, it's 1512 First Street."

They turned and walked to a waiting buggy. The driver clicked the reins along the horse's back and they were off. Margret stood looking after them for the longest while then went on about her work. If it had been Leo's father, she wouldn't have told them where he was at.

The buggy pulled to a stop in front of a plain brown one story building with open double doors facing the street. Both men got down, with a rifle and holster in their hands. Mister Patterson told the driver to wait. Walking in, he saw Leo and another young fellow putting a forge together.

"Hello Leo, you look well." He handed over the rifle and holster, smiling as he did so.

"As do you Grandfather, what brings you to Colorado?"

"That rifle and holster you came up with, now that is quite the contraption. Will you tell me what took place between you and your father down in Chloride, New Mexico? He was rather upset upon his return to Patterson."

"Yes Sir, and I'd bet he is a lot more upset right about now. It is dinner time, why don't we go down to the café and eat while we talk? I'm hungry as all get out."

"Yes, that would be fine."

Leo looked over at David. "Want to come along?"

"Naw y'all go ahead. I'll lock up and just go on back home and eat dinner with Margret."

Leo held the door for his grandfather and the other man then followed them to a table. They ordered their meal and drank ice tea while waiting. "Well Son, what happened?"

Leo told everything, from the conception of the rifle and holster, to his father being put on the stage by the local sheriff. "That's about it Grandpa, and we came here to Denver and have our shop where we will make the rifles and holsters. James Catron and Sherry P Thompson Catron are very good lawyers, don't you think?"

Grandpa smiled, "Yes I sure do. They made that bunch back home eat crow. If your father hadn't canceled that contract, would you have really sued and prosecuted?"

"Yes Sir, if that is what it took to get my gun back and away from father. Grandpa, James said you were bringing a new contract. You know I will never sign it, nor will David."

"Splendid! Well that concludes my business in Denver. I will be on the evening train back to New Jersey."

"You mean you are not going to try and get me to change my mind?"

"Certainly not! I think you will do rather well on your own. From what I saw a few minutes ago, I'd say you have yourself a good partner. Is there any message you want me to give your mother? She did ask about you."

"Just that I hope she is well. Grandpa, I know I still owe you five thousand dollars and will pay you as soon as I can."

"No need my boy, think no more about it. That was a gift well used. I am happy you got out of New Jersey and found your own way. If you had stayed, you might have turned out just like your father. And you are right, David and Margret and the people of Chloride are more family than what you have back in New Jersey. All of these people care for you deeply. You now have a good life, so live it and be happy. My boy, I do wish you well. Goodbye and perhaps we will see one another before I get old and die."

"I would like that Grandpa, yes I would."

Within the next two weeks, they only had one rifle finished and just a bit more than half of another. "David, this is not working out very well. I thought with the both of us, we could do it. But it is just taking too long. We have to get hold of enough money to buy machinery. Tomorrow we'll go to the bank and see about a loan."

That evening as they ate supper, Margret saw how down hearted they were. "While I do dishes and get the kitchen cleaned, why don't y'all go down to the saloon and have a few beers? You both have been working too hard and need a break."

David looked over at Leo. "What do you think?"

"Yeah, I could use a good cold beer or two. But we'll go to the hotel and not one of those bars where we could be mugged."

They had not finished their first beer, as they did more talking than drinking. Just as David started to call for another round, in walked Dick Boggs. He stood, "Hey Dick, over here."

As Dick headed that way, Leo asked who in the heck is that? "You'll see, and be darned sure surprised." He stayed standing and stuck out his hand for a shake. "Dick, this is my partner, Leo."

"Howdy Leo, mind if I sit?"

"Naw, go right ahead."

David called for three beers then asked what Dick was doing back in Denver. "Picking up some stuff for the ranch."

"Did your wife come with you?"

"Naw, she didn't feel much like a quick trip. How's that invention of y'alls coming along?"

"Bout stalled out for the present. We had to pull the contract and are trying to build them ourselves."

"How's that working out?"

"It's not, without the proper machinery, we won't be able to make more than three or so a month. Make a slim living is all that would do. But we'll not give up, we'll do er."

"Why don't you just get the machinery?"

"Money, it takes money and lot of it."

Dick thought a minute. "Yeah, like how much money?"

David looked over at Leo. Leo smiled, "A lot more than we have. "I'd say for everything, a complete shop would run anywhere from fifteen to twenty thousand dollars. Yeah and on top of that another thousand or so for signs and advertizing will be needed. We're going to try the bank tomorrow."

Dick ordered another round of beer before asking, "Would another partner with money help?"

"What kind of partner and what kind of split?"

"Say for thirty thousand dollars you'd give ten per-cent of the profit on all sales."

Leo and David looked at one another, both shaking their heads up and down. That sounds good to us. Are you going to be in town tomorrow?"

"Yeah I can't leave for another couple of days."

"Alright, in the morning at nine we'll all go over to the Catron and Thompson law office and have a contract drawn up."

The next morning they talked with Sherry and Jim. Sherry smiled and said, "Alright, y'all find something to do for about an hour so I can get this thing drawn up."

They walked over to the bank, where Dick transferred thirty thousand dollars to David and Leo's account. Within the hour they were back in front of Sherry.

"Now before you sign this, let me make sure I have it right. All money from sales will go into David and Leo's joint account. Then of that ten per-cent will be transferred to Mrs. Garrison's account until thirty thousand dollars has been transferred. Then after the thirty thousand, the ten per-cent will go into the Dick Boggs' account. Is all of that correct?"

"Yes, except the ten per-cent is only off the profits."

"I have no way of knowing what the profits are and

what is not. It is all money to me. That will be up to your bookkeeper. And if you don't have one, you will before long." All three boys looked at each other with Leo saying. "Yeah, we'll figure that out."

They all signed the contract, stood and shook hands, then with Sherry. "Thank you Ma'am."

They walked out with David saying, "Dick, why don't you drop by the house for supper tonight. My wife is a great little cook."

Dick walked off to check on the ranch's order and Leo and David walked back to the shop. As they walked along Leo said, "Man was it luck we ran into a friend of your or not? I don't even know if we could have gotten money from the bank."

They opened the shop and went to work. After a bit David said, "Leo, you know how I've always said everything happens for a reason. You know, like you coming to a little out of the way town in New Mexico and us becoming friends."

"Yeah so, what does all of this have to do with that?"

"Dick Boggs was riding with the boy that shot Margret and that is what started the whole thing of me needing a new gun."

Leo stopped and turned to face David. "You have got to be joking!"

"Nope, but as you can tell he is not the kind of man to shoot no one. He isn't even getting any of that ten per-cent. He's giving it to Mrs. Garrison and those kids she feeds."

Leo stood there a moment just looking straight at him. "Good Lord, stop and think David. Just look at how many lives this new gun has already touched and changed. We will never have to worry about money again and Mrs. Garrison will be able to feed more kids than ever before. You are right, stuff happens for a reason. Some very good things, some very bad."

About The Author

Paul L. Thompson was born and raised in the southwest and has traveled horseback over most of the locations he writes about. Over twenty years of research goes into his novels. Every location used in the author's novels is true. None of his characters have been written to death by other authors and he uses language as was used in the old west.

Thompson is now retired and writes full time. His novels are a series with the same main characters and once in a while he will bring back a sub-character. M D Thompson is the author's hero and is a little U S Marshall. That is his name, M D, no period after either letter. Every novel is a complete story. Some of the characters come from research the author did on his own family and this is where some of the stories come from.

Thompson's readers range in age from the forties and to the middle eighties. He receives a tremendous amount of fan mail and will gladly share some with anyone who is interested.

Visit his website at:
http://www.oldwestnovels.com
or write him at paullt@isp.com

CPSIA information can be obtained at www.ICGtesting.com
Printed in the USA
LVOW130101090812

293561LV00001B/8/P